Potomac Review

Potomac Review

EDITOR

Albert Kapikian

MANAGING EDITOR	POETRY EDITOR	NONFICTION EDITOR
Monica Mische	Katherine Smith	Viola Clune

ADMINISTRATIVE ASSISTANT/WEBMASTER

Om B. Rusten

ASSOCIATE EDITORS

Caleb Berer	Robert Giron	Mike Maggio
Conrad Berger	Jessie Gouveneur	Edwin McCleskey
Anjennee Cannon	Heather Levine	David Saitzeff
Theron Coleman	Michael LeBlanc	Jessie Seigel
Fox Dietz	Kateema Lee	Jen Smith
Hieu Duong	Alejandro Leopardi	Ellen Sullivan
Courtney Ford	David Lott	Marianne Szlyk

INTERNS

David Berger and Allan Bernal

Potomac Review is a journal of fiction, poetry, and nonfiction published by the Paul Peck Humanities Institute at Montgomery College, Rockville
51 Mannakee Street, Rockville, MD 20850

Potomac Review has been made possible through the generosity of Montgomery College.

A special thanks to Dean Elizabeth Benton.

For submission guidelines and more information:
www.potomacreview.org

Potomac Review, Inc. is a not-for-profit 501 c(3) corp.
Member, Council of Literary Magazines & Presses
Indexed by the American Humanities Index
ISBN:979-8-9858514-3-6 ISSN: 1073-1989

SUBSCRIBE TO POTOMAC REVIEW
One year at $24 (2 issues)
Two years at $36 (4 issues)
Sample copy order, $12 (single issue)

COVER PHOTOGRAPH

ROCHELLE COHEN

"The Other"

Table of Contents

POETRY

MEDITATIONS

POSTSCRIPT

A RECONCILIATORY APPROACH

THE new heresy is to assume good faith, but since *Potomac Review* comes out of a community college, where we have no principle of sorting, where there is, at least in some rudimentary form, the necessary, if not sufficient, condition for a commons, we have no choice but to listen, and learn from people who cannot so easily draw boundaries, who cannot so readily choose to live inside their own contrivances, people for whom the world gets in, for whom the world, therefore—because they are people forced to listen to, and learn from, *the other*—is not yet passe. A heresy was never a falsehood but a truth improperly amplified, but now that there are no common truths, a reconciliatory approach, though extolled in principle, is forbidden in practice, and the community college, though reproduced in almost every county in every state, the only place, de facto, where we all still sit with one another, where a coming together across all lines of demarcation still exists, is relegated to the unseen.

We are not naïve to hidden motives behind calls to *just come together,* how it often serves the fig leaf of bipartisanship, a stalking horse and pretext for discriminatory and/or market forces, and how, in the same way, there are often unspoken and unexamined ideologies behind calls for a supposedly neutral and hidden muse. We have become self-conscious of the historicity of our assumptions and so calling for a reconciliatory approach is itself a call for an ethically engaged aesthetics, a choice of course, and the tragedy that choice implies, is that there are other choices that could just as easily have been argued for and made. But since *Potomac Review* comes out of a community college, the course is already made for us. Riffing on Gayatri Chakravorty Spivak's formulation, at least as to its cadence, here we are "learning to learn" from each other and see in our principle of non-sorting Amy Clampitt's "region, / a weather and a point of view / as yet unsettled" where we are forced to see, not separate, and in this kind of seeing present an American form of writing that lives only in its reconciliatory role.

Whether or not the country, and the literature coming out of the country, must move towards reconciliation, at *our* community college, often noted as the most diverse in the continental United States, the necessary conditions already exist to model such love and attention to the other, and while the terms of our existence were not chosen, but given, we have learned from being in such a condition, learned to love its terms despite the enigmas those terms present. It is now our aspiration to create not only the necessary, but the sufficient conditions, setting out to accomplish them by asking questions, not giving answers, opening, not closing doors, hoping to learn about reconciliation from groups who cannot be so quick to draw boundaries, who cannot so quickly withdraw into spaces of separation.

Trading in the world for our common disgust with each other— click *like* has, as they say in business schools, "gone to scale"—our "friendships" are now often based on the pledge to hate the same people. Our apathy with respect to *the other,* therefore, has been socially engineered, so anything that goes against click *like* is rooted out, the social good left out of "social" media, its algorithms designed to enrage, not engage, or if engage, to limit, blanket, filter our experience, and feed it back to us because it is *calculated* for us to like. We are aware that literature for the common good is often bad—inferior literature, as they say, is always written with the best of motives—but when commitment to the common good is heresy, aesthetic values are subordinated to click *like*, the literature is even worse, the parts of the poem fit too easily together, you always know what's coming, and a stranger never approaches. There is no commons, just a sense of insulation, *calculated* insulation. It is no wonder our click *like* aesthetic is intimately connected with disembodied, socially disconnected forms of intelligence; we cannot automate moral responsibility or an ethic of care when there is nothing at stake. Human intelligence is not just about bond trading—whether Nick Carraway's in F. Scott Fitzgerald's *The Great Gatsby*, or Benjamin Rask's/Andrew Bevel's in "Harold Vanner's" *Bonds,* the novel within a novel in Hernan Diaz's *Trust.* We are not just systems, but also embodied individuals, and though immensely vulnerable to the education of desire, we are also capable of social intelligence and moral reasoning, because we are living in a society with other people where our actions have consequences for the other, the unseen.

Where is the writer today who, rather than using words, is used by words? Now we have a set of ideas and norms that says, even for American poets, if another's suffering goes against our shared vision, it goes against *us.* If our knowledge is only our perspective, and *the other* is not included in it, then the literature of reconciliation, of the transcendence of difference, is impossible. Each side has speech codes, but the greater threat, for a poet, is to choose one side *or* the other, because for a poet a speech code is machinery, addicted to results, and in those results the other is never *also-I.* The initial seed of inspiration brings with it restraint and empathy, humility, and gratitude for *whomever* is abroad, and the decision to share does not include the decision to disqualify, for the decision to share is by definition reconciliatory; the poet will never meet but even a small percentage of their readers.

Taking from the cover title of this issue, we are calling for a series of themed issues to explore this reconciliatory approach, beginning with *The Other,* in Spring 2025, and, in Fall 2025, *The Unseen.* Like othering, *not seeing* is also a choice. We are not the only ones who observe and perhaps even engage in forms of mimesis. Just as self implies other, the seen implicates the unseen. Much *can* be seen and understood, but there is an ever-vanishing horizon, and the other, and the unseen, call into this future. Seeing and failure to see are literary matters, and while our themed issues will be capacious enough to allow for each writer's vision—transgressive, disruptive, queer, representative of the animal turn in the Anthropocene—they will be defining enough to proscribe that vision into the form of a task, an aesthetic task, where literature is itself seen as a form of reconciliation that does not recognize otherness, difference, dis-figuration, or boundaries *except as* an also-I where the unseen is that aspect of artistic creation that is ahead of its time, that reveals itself as what has *not yet* been seen.

We do not know what the literature is that will meet our moment, that will be seen as ahead of its time, but we have a few guiding principles, coming, as we do, out of a community college, a "system" engineered for the common good—a place, a region, where the opportunity to lead a life of the mind is made available to everyone, a paradisal, magical place amidst the ruins, like Psyche's palace in C.S. Lewis's *Till We Have Faces*, often deliberately unseen, but like yeast injected into the mass, a place where the preconditions for the solution to our country's predicament perhaps already exist because partaking of the new heresy by looking at, living in, and leaving the door open to the opposite interpretations held by *the other*.

We are aware that the old liberal universalism has been rejected as requiring essentialist categories—even as "strategic essentialism" has been embraced as the road to justice—but to think and act collectively will require sharing, a crossing out of boundaries, even "strategic" ones. The other is ever and only a representation of the other, the real other is *wholly other*, so the task of the literature of reconciliation is to comprehend this other in the incomprehensibility in which it presents itself, the other the mystery which we want to comprehend because it is *also-I;* and if not now, when that other may also include our burning planet, when?

Literature imagined as a place for imagined futures, where the other is also-I, where the seen implicates the unseen, is of course nothing new. The photograph of a heron on our cover, taken at Greenbelt Lake, part of Greenbelt, Maryland, one of the three still extant community-owned "Greenbelt Towns" (the other two Greendale, Wisconsin and Greenhills, Ohio) conceived by FDR in 1935, could be a kind of emblem of the style of the literature of reconciliation, as Erich Auerbach, in *Mimesis*, called Odysseus' scar an emblem of the Homeric style. The photograph itself is, of course, mimetic, and renders the idea of reconciliation with the other recognizable, suggesting a plain-to-see sameness amidst conspicuous difference and disfiguration. While photographs depict reality, they are also a reading of reality, mirroring the represent-ations of reality in its eyewitnesses, who provide their own contexts. The *green* in "Greenbelt towns" referred to their belts of green space, the towns both text and context, not big box places, tens of thousands of which now dot our country where the text and context are the same, but text and context as a presence and a style in the form of a recurring motif for an imagined future—not lifeless, artificial, but letting the encounter with the stranger tell us what the other and the unseen mean, letting ourselves be told, even as we are telling, shown, as we are showing—*this* the event, *this* the plot, and on our cover, *this* the scene implicating the unseen.

As editors of themed issues, questions, not answers, will guide our task, questions of a certain kind—probing for connectedness, and rejecting those that lead to boundary making, generating a form of aesthetic criticism that will require not only the usual perspicacity but a rich and receptive heart that, as for its scholarship, will be inwardly amateur, because beginning in reverence and love will see potentiality, and a horizon, open to a series of revelatory future-facing awakenings where one day the only disqualification will be the act of disqualifying the *other,* the *unseen.* We hope to learn how to reject any aesthetics of human disqualification and in pursuing a reconciliatory approach for its own sake, where, instead of boundary drawing, taking note of where the light travels, and following that light, the Mid-Atlantic light, itself also text and context, center and periphery, holding and surrounding the heron of Greenbelt Lake.

In the end, a willingness to look for common ground is part of the American imagination, for the only form of imagination that matters, for American literature and the American commons, is moral imagination, the ability, that is, to walk in someone else's shoes. Our experiment in self-government belongs, in the end, to the world of the human spirit, and with respect to the other, and to the unseen, literature is a way of assembling them, and the depth and power and voice of those assembled materials will always be in inverse proportion to how deeply their lives are buried, that is, how far out of sight. To have a legislator reach across the aisle, creating in himself or herself the other that he or she is seeing, is a heresy now, even though any "vision" that does not include the other labors under the mistake that including the other is inconsistent with moral force when, in fact, it is the very font of moral force. Like literary epiphanies, the other provides an ontological opening: the great legislator, like the great artist interrogates him or herself and knows that while the love of others must be boundless, the love of self is demonstrated in self-criticism, brought into its heresy by the other, the unseen.

RACHMONES

MY father and I drove up to Hull to go flounder fishing even though he hated fishing and I hated him. I had just turned twelve so maybe it was a birthday present or maybe he thought it would take my mind off the fact that my parents had just split up, my mom running off with my father's former best friend, the guy I'd grown up calling Uncle Jim. The guy who taught me how to fish when my father was too busy shut up in his office with his accounting. I wasn't angry at my mom for choosing Jim. I was angry that they didn't take me with them.

My father and I spent the first day on the small center console boat he rented. He knew his way around boats a bit because he grew up spending summers on the Jersey shore fishing with Jim. We were fishing for flounder with live sandworms that my father didn't know or couldn't remember how to hook. I showed him as we drifted across Quincy Bay. Jim had taught me well: you run the hook through one worm, in one end, out the other. You add another worm on the end for good measure so it dangles and looks delicious to any curious fish.

"See?" I said, holding my newly-baited hook in my father's face. He looked squeamish. Whether from the rock of the boat or the worm twirling in its death throes in front of him, I didn't know. I didn't care. I just wanted to show him what I could do. And to watch him squirm.

"Is this the way Jim taught you to fish?"

"We'd spend the whole day out here, start bright and early, me and Jim and mom. Mom would always make bologna and Swiss sandwiches on kaiser rolls with tons of coarse grain German mustard. And we'd listen to music sometimes too." I remembered how they'd dance together towards the end of the day. I'd sit in the back of the boat, one eye on the lines, waiting for a hit, the other on them, as they laughed and danced in tight circles in the bow. "Sometimes Jim would let me sip his beer," I said.

"It sounds like you had fun out here. With them."

"Here. This pole's all set up for you. Drop the line off the bow." I turned to set up a pole for myself.

We spent the day fishing mostly in silence. The radio on the boat was barely audible and my father hadn't thought to bring a boombox. Jim usually did that. But the silence wasn't the only thing wrong with the scene. Jim looked like he belonged on a boat, a working-class Kennedy. He was lean and tan, shaggy blonde hair pouring out of a beat-up Mets cap. My father looked like a Jewish Al Gore: stuffy, dull, and too weak to contest the election everyone said he won last year. Al Gore with a bigger schnoz and a kippah that looked like a bright white bald spot. My father was all wrong. He looked lost behind the wheel, bored with the rod in his hand, and spent most of the day mooning over the sea like a Romantic poet. I hated him more and more. Some birthday present.

My father had also forgotten to pack us lunches so we shared the bag of chips I'd bought at the bait shop. He told me to wash my hands so I wouldn't get sandworm guts on the chips and I said it was part of the flavoring. My father scrunched up his face and I said, "Don't get your panties in a bunch," and his face scrunched even more, like it was collapsing in on itself. It was one of Jim's favorite lines and I knew it would wound my father to hear it. I grabbed another fistful of chips with my grimy hands.

WE ate a half mushroom, half pepperoni pizza in the motel for dinner. Or whatever passes for pizza in Hull, Mass. I'd dragged my father to Sandy's, a dive bar across the street from our motel on the barb of Hull's hook-shaped peninsula. The fish and chips were famous at Sandy's but my father didn't like the look of the place. He took one look at the faded Confederate flag hanging over the jukebox and said we were having pizza instead. I'd never noticed it before and wasn't sure what the Confederacy was doing in the heart of Yankeedom but I didn't much care. The décor didn't affect the fish and chips. But my father insisted. So, we ate our pizza on our respective twin beds. My father delicately ate two slices from the mushroom side in the same amount of time it took me to polish off the rest of the pie. I chucked the empty box in the corner and a piece of half-gnawed crust leapt out of the box and landed on the worn-out carpet. I ignored it, flipping through channels on the tv. My father had been watching some suits talk about Bush's tax cuts but I wanted to find reruns of MacGyver. I admired MacGyver. He could fix anything with some tape and his Swiss army knife. Maybe he could even fix my father? I usually watched the show with Jim and my mom. Or I watched it alone when they went out for a drive.

"Are you going to pick that up?" My father asked, raising his voice slightly to be heard over the hum of the a/c in the window and the snippets of news and canned applause coming from the television.

"Nope."

"Why not?"

"Jim says it creates jobs."

"Leaving an empty pizza box on the floor creates jobs?"

I nodded, keeping my eyes on the tv. *The Rugrats* was on and I liked the show but didn't want to seem like some stupid kid so I kept searching.

"Maybe it doesn't create work but just creates more work for someone who's probably already working too hard."

"How's that my problem?"

My father took off his glasses, rubbed the bridge of his nose. "Do you know rachmones?"

"Metal band?" I said, wiping my greasy fingers on the blanket.

"No. It's Yiddish."

I shrugged. I didn't know any Yiddish. My father dropped a word here and there and I heard an occasional Yiddish insult on *Seinfeld* but I had no interest in all that Jewish stuff. Neither had my mom. We both thought it sounded silly and looked it too. The little goofy hats, the strings hanging from the guys' shirts in the Kosher deli in Fairlawn my father dragged us to a couple of times a year when he felt he needed to reconnect to some culture we didn't understand. Or maybe he just liked the pastrami? I didn't care. It wasn't for me. It wasn't something I recognized as mine.

"It means have a little sympathy. Have a little mercy, a little pity."

"For who? The maid? Isn't cleaning up the place part of her job?"

"It is. But there's no reason to make her job harder."

I turned the tv off. "Why are you like this?"

"Like what?" He said, looking genuinely confused. And weak. Or kind. I couldn't tell the difference back then.

"I need to get some air," I said, borrowing my mom's favorite exit line. Though in the end she needed more than just air. She needed Florida. She needed Jim. She needed to free herself of us. I jumped off the bed, put on my sneakers, and opened the door.

"It's late. Don't go too far."

"Don't get your panties in a bunch," I said, opening the door to the motel parking lot and the hot July night.

"What's wrong?"

"Al fucking Gore," I yelled, slamming the door behind me.

I WALKED across the street to the phonebooth outside Sandy's. I'd been there a dozen times with my mom and Jim. Last summer I even had lunch there myself while Jim and my mom ran some errands.

I called them at their new place in Florida. They moved down there in the spring and had bought a place not far from the water. They even had a little boat and had gone fishing for marlin. I was supposed to visit this summer but something came up, they cancelled, and I was stuck in a motel learning Yiddish from an Al Gore lookalike instead.

My mom picked up on the seventh ring, mid-laugh.

"Hi mom, it's me," I said.

"Hi sweetie," she said, her voice warm and soft like she'd had a few drinks. "What's the word?"

"I'm in Hull. With my father."

"Are the fish biting?"

"Father couldn't catch a fish if it bit him in the ass."

She laughed, then said something I couldn't catch to someone near her.

"What?"

"I was talking to one of Jim's friends. He has a ton of friends down here already. You know how sociable he is. We're having a little party."

"Do you think I could visit next month, then?"

"What?"

"Maybe I could visit next month?" I said, a little embarrassed by how needy I sounded. I looked through the greasy glass doors of the phonebooth but no one was around to hear me.

"Next month? Hm. I don't know if that'll work."

"Why not? This month didn't work. You can't leave me in Jersey with father for the whole summer. You can't," I said, crying all of sudden.

"Don't get your panties in a bunch, dear," she said and I heard laughter in the background.

The line went dead. I was out of quarters. I walked back to the motel. From across the road, I saw the door to our room was open, my father standing watch at the threshold until I'd safely crossed the street.

THE next day was nearly as bad as the first. My father caught nothing and the only fish I hauled up was a sea robin. Little bottom feeding monsters that Jim called "trash fish." My father liked the look of it, though. He said it was "interesting." I said I wasn't interested in his opinion. But he at least knew how to bait his own hook now and seemed more confident at the helm. And he remembered to pack lunch, too. Thick slices of Hebrew National salami on bagels slathered with spicy brown mustard. No Swiss, but tasty.

Aside from my interesting sea robin, we caught nothing the rest of the day. My father took me to Sandy's for dinner. I'd talked the place up. Practically pleaded. The fish and chips. The jukebox. My father wanted to sit at a booth but I preferred the bar. We usually sat at the bar, Jim and mom and me. So, we sat at the bar, me in my old, sandworm-gut-covered jean shorts, my father in a polo and chinos he pressed in the motel with an iron the woman at the front desk lent him. As usual, he looked ridiculous, even more so at Sandy's.

I ate my fish and chips and most of my father's. He smiled weakly, shifting on the rickety stool and keeping his elbows off the sticky bar. Some oaf on his way back from the bathroom bumped into him, spinning my father on his stool.

"Watch where you're going, pal," the man said.

"Watch yourself," I said, balling my fists and knowing he wouldn't have dared bump into Jim like that.

My father looked mortified and apologized to the bruiser. The man went to his friends at the end of the bar, pointed at us, said something, and they all laughed. I stood up and my father said, "Let it go, son. There aren't enough hours in the day to fight every schmuck you come across."

"I need to get some air," I said. I glared at the clowns at the end of the bar as I went outside. I didn't realize I was calling my mom until I was already in the phone booth listening to the line ringing in Florida a thousand miles away.

Jim picked up on the second ring. "Jim, hi. It's me. You'll never guess where I am," I said. "I'm in the phonebooth outside Sandy's."

"Hey, buddy. That's great. Hull in July. You must be reeling them in like crazy."

"Just a sea robin today. My father is bad luck."

"A sea robin? Yeah, that may be. He was never much of a fisherman. A hell of an accountant though," he said with a laugh.

"Jim, is my mom there? Maybe I could talk with her. Yesterday we were talking about me coming down there next month but the line went dead."

"Down here, you say? Well, she's actually busy at the moment."

"Busy?"

I didn't hear anything for a minute like he'd covered the phone with his hand. "I mean, she's out. Food shopping, I think."

"Food shopping? At nine pm?"

"I'll have her call you tomorrow. I've got to go, buddy. Happy fishing," he said.

He hung up before I could tell him that she didn't have my number. I whispered "rachmones" into the telephone though I knew no one was listening.

OUR third and final day on the boat went better. We fell into a rhythm, my father and I, and kept out of each other's way. But still we caught nothing all morning. In the afternoon, my father said we should give up on the flounder and try for striped bass. A man in the marina said they might be biting. I preferred fishing for stripers anyway because I'd rather cast and reel than just wait for something along the bottom to strike the line.

We hit a school of stripers the minute we changed bait. Small flashes of silver and black leaping out of the water as we reeled them in. It was fun. They put up a good fight. My father even caught one large enough to keep.

"And Jim said you were never much of a fisherman," I said, marveling at his catch.

"Did he? What else did he say?"

I looked at my father, this accountant of the open seas, and told him some of what I'd heard over the years. That he was kind, too kind, my mom had said. That she found this kindness unattractive. That he was reliable, Jim had said. And reliably wimpy. That he was too Jewy, they'd both said, leaving me to wonder if there was a right amount of Jewy-ness. I told him of the laughs they'd had at his expense. About how I laughed along with them and suddenly I was furious not at my father but for him.

"That's enough," he said, looking pale but grimly determined too. "Do you want to keep this one?"

I stared at the fish dangling from the line over the side of the boat, wrenched from its world, suffocating, while freedom was a mere foot below it. I shook my head.

"Me neither. It's better to let them go."

I held the line while my father removed the hook and released the fish back into the water. Together we watched it shimmer swiftly away from the boat.

AFTER we docked, hosed down the boat, and returned the keys to the man in the marina, my father turned to me, smiled, and said, "Sandy's?"

I nodded and we drove back to Sandy's, not even stopping at the motel for my father to shower and change.

We sat at the bar again. Ordered fish and chips. My father ordered a beer though he rarely drank. He even pushed it towards me, said I could take a sip.

I picked the bottle up, looked at the busty blonde in lederhosen on the label, and put it down again. "No, thanks. I never really liked it anyway," I said.

"Me neither."

"They used to dance here," I said. "Mom and Jim."

"I know."

"I'm sorry," I said, admitting to myself that they did a lot more than dance on these fishing trips. That maybe I was culpable, too, as their pretext, nothing but a cover story. Maybe that's all I ever was to them. I started to cry.

"Do you need to get some air?" My dad asked.

I shook my head and stayed on the stool beside my dad. He rested his hand on my shoulder, lightly, as I cried. He didn't remove it until someone bumped into him again. Slammed into him is more like it. He leaned into me and I felt the shock of the impact too.

"Kike," I heard someone say.

I saw the man from yesterday. The bruiser must have been one of Sandy's regulars. My dad's face went white. A bead of sweat trembled on his lip in the shadow of his nose.

The bruiser smirked at us then turned and continued towards his friends at the end of the bar.

"Kike?" I asked. "Is that Yiddish too?"

My dad shook his head, slowly stood, and walked towards the end of the bar to catch the man before he sat down. He tapped him on the shoulder. The man turned, grinning. And my dad punched him square in that grin. With disbelief and fear and pride, I watched the wind-up, my dad's thin and sunburned right arm cocking back, his small fist dangling for a moment in the air as if it couldn't quite believe what it was about to do, before launching forward into the meat of some stranger's face. Only, unlike in the movies where the Nazis are laid out by a single of Indiana Jones's punches, the man didn't stop grinning. His head barely moved. Maybe Al Gore was right, after all? Maybe some fights are unwinnable. I kept watching as the man grabbed my dad's shirt with his left hand and with his right repeatedly punched him in the face, hook after hook, flattening his once proud schnoz. My dad fell to the floor, his kippah crumpled on the floor like a used Kleenex, his face and shirt smeared with blood and snot. The floor bloody too. Just as the man raised his boot to stomp my dad into the ground—a boot which seemed to multiply there above him, becoming a dozen boots, a million, my mother's, Jim's, George W. Bush's, countless soles looming over us—I threw myself across my dad yelling "rachmones, rachmones, rachmones," over and over again. Though I doubted a word no one understood would shield us, I didn't know what else to say.

THE FIRST CONCEIT

Eve discovered Adam had already bit the apple. He had eaten
the whole thing. This was the first lie man told woman.
The surprise on his face at the taste of her offering was well put-on,
but he had given himself away when he swept her hair
away from her breast before the bite, not after.
And, oh, that apple. The sweet flesh. The give of the skin.
The feeling of teeth sliding in, juice down the throat,
nectar on the chin. Beautiful fruit. First love. Splendid glory.
Globe opening like the unfurled world about them. And God in Heaven
borrowing from Pan, sowed mischief in the form of this test.
Adam and Eve's devotion tested by curiosity sewn
into their muscles like embroidery. Adam smiled with chagrin
when she discovered him, and then he was bold.
He placed his hand on her head like a dog attempting dominance.
And Eve, knowing all that he knew and more, she knelt.
Let him have it, she thought. She had seen his deception
and with it the end. She would watch. And wait.

PANTOUM

My mother asks, *What is a poem?*
A sentence broken into shorter lines?
Meter, syllables, it doesn't need to rhyme?
Psalms, Song of Solomon, not Leviticus.

A sentence broken into shorter lines?
A place to enter, space for feeling and breath
Psalms, Song of Solomon, not Leviticus
a garden of fallen apples, honeyed wasps

a place to enter, space for feeling and breath
nothing measured, but the measure of a measure
a garden of fallen apples, honeyed wasps
the blessing of two ponies in a pasture

nothing measured, but the measure of a measure
Meter, syllables, it doesn't need to rhyme?
the blessing of two ponies in a pasture
My mother asks, *What is a poem?*

TWO HOURS

THEY had spent three days under the rubble, and during that time her mistake of letting the dog get fat suddenly became an asset. The warmth emanating from Silas's back, which was pressed against her left side, countered the coldness of her urine-soaked jogging pants that first night. Gradually the pants dried out, and as the time passed, needing to relieve herself ceased to be a problem.

It wasn't that she didn't like to exercise. She had run two half marathons, one in her home city of Boston and one during her semester abroad in London. But Silas was more of a lolly-gagger. He liked to walk a few steps and then stop and sniff what looked like nothing to her for an impossibly long time. "That blade of grass," her friend Agnes explained once, "is his Instagram." But Lila wasn't a stroller, or a scroller, and more often than not her desire for a run took precedence over Silas's need for a 45-minute meander.

Silas didn't seem to mind. And in all other respects—aloofness, waking hour, noise level, the occasional need for cuddling, and the number of times a day he needed to pee–they agreed completely. He was her companion, not too needy and fully committed, the way a good dog should be. But without regular walks, in a few years she had an obese Golden Retriever mix sharing her bed.

She had started to walk him more just before the building collapsed though the effects were yet to be seen. On the coldest days, she would chuckle at Silas patiently waiting at the apartment door while she layered herself in snow pants, a fleece, a puffer jacket, a neck-gaiter and hat, and gloves under mittens. She got so cold ambling at such slow speeds. Yet there stood Silas, with his unironic gaze, in the same seamless fur coat he wore year round, ready to face the elements.

She learned to become interested in his rambling. Most of the walk he spent with his nose to the ground. Sometimes he would sniff under the corridors of bent grasses with the exuberance of a lover in the curves of their beloved's body. He would then jump high and pounce with both front paws and come up with a tiny, panicked pygmy shrew or meadow vole, which he would carry for a few yards after its capture, set down, nose once in its wet, creased middle, then leave woefully behind as she tugged him away. Dogs could smell a single drop of liquid, she had seen on a poster at the vet's, in a body of water as large as twenty Olympic-sized swimming pools. Their noses had up to three-hundred-million olfactory receptors, compared to humans' six million.

Once, on a walk, Silas had looked up for a second, and the full sturgeon moon, a supermoon that year, caught his eye. He stayed transfixed, in a pose not impossible for his species but also not usual—dogs don't spend a ton of time looking at the sky. There he stood, neck craned upward, seemingly enamored, gazing at the spectacularly large moon as if he were Homer or Sappho.

That summer, she and Agnes had taken Silas with them to Agnes' parents' cabin in the Berkshires for a weekend and she had been amazed at the many hours he spent sniffing and hunting along the forest's edge, catching nothing 95% of the time but persisting, nevertheless. It was as if his usual, apartment-dwelling, hobbit-like self were a farce. When he finally scampered up onto the deck where they sat eating lunch and made eye contact with them, wagging his tail gently, Agnes looked down into his amber-colored eyes which evolution had trained him to keep on her face.

"It looks like he loves us," she said. But really he just wants a hamburger."

THE building had collapsed three years earlier. Afterwards, she threw herself into work and therapy, eventually just work. Her job as an accountant required a kind of non–abstract hyper focus that was in itself a sort of therapy. She thought about the collapse once a day, every morning upon waking, as she did on this morning, as she felt Silas's warmth against her in the bed, just as she had felt it for those entire three dark days, while the calories burned off of both of them and her mind lived an entire other life she had neither prepared for nor desired, until the firefighters finally heard Silas's whimper and her weak, crazed *help* and brought in their drills and axes and jaws of life and pulled them both out and wrapped them in those crinkly emergency blankets and gave them water and energy bars.

There had been international newspaper articles about the rescue, of course—three days is a long time to remain under all that concrete on a succession of cold Boston nights. Some reported her unconscious, and exaggerated Silas's bark, making the dog Lassie-like in his efforts for both to be rescued. It was the kind of story everyone likes, one punctuating mark of survival at the end of a very long sentence of unimaginable horror.

She let herself think about the collapse only once a day, and then as the therapist had encouraged, left it all behind for the other 23 hours and 59 minutes, until it would rise up inside her again the next morning just as she gained consciousness, as she felt Silas's warmth, as she woke up, first feeling traumatized, and then relieved, and then happy, and then guilty. Ninety-eight people had died in that building collapse. Three had survived. And also Silas.

On this day the waking guilt was shrouded by an incredible headache. She managed to pop two Advil from a value sized container she kept in the nightstand, and which she took for menstrual cramps once a month. She didn't normally get headaches. She hoped the Advil would last through her meeting at 9:00.

Silas leaped from the bed when he heard the nightstand drawer open. He stood at the bedside, eyes fixed on her eyes, tail pointed straight out, wagging it a hair to the left and right when she glanced at him, let her gaze rest on him for a moment.

"Good morning," she managed to say, reaching down to cup his snout in her hand, rub the fluffy fur on his chest, a gesture she had read made dogs feel proud, and then gently tug each of his ears, something he tolerated but didn't seem to particularly like, just so she could enjoy their velvety feel. "It's time for your walk, I suppose." Christ, through her pounding temple, she could hardly get the words out.

She walked him every day now, twice a day, and it showed. He'd gone from 65 pounds to 45 pounds, an acceptable weight for a dog of his breed and stature, and maintained it for the past two years. She'd grown to enjoy the walks. It was true; they were both pack animals and walking together, even in the city with a leash binding them, even with his occasional stubbornness and her occasional impolite tug to get him moving, had cemented their bond.

She pushed the covers off and rose out of bed, but as she did so her headache became unbearable. She vomited, reached for the bed to sit down again but missed and hit her head on the corner of the nightstand as she thumped to the floor. Head wounds, she had read once, but wasn't thinking now, bled a lot. A pool of pulpy syrupy blood began to form like a shadow, the wrong shadow, behind her temple.

Silas walked back and forth alongside her body a few times. He licked her on the nose. He barked once, softly. He lay down beside her, sphynx-style: his hips unrelaxed, ready to jump into action.

He waited two hours.

Then, when he could smell the putricine and cadaverine of her decaying body—dogs can pick up this scent within minutes of a death or as much as decades later–he began to lap up the blood until he was so close to her head he was licking the wound itself, his incisors hitting the soft wrapping of flesh around her skull, her scalp-hairs looping his tongue, so that when Agnes retrieved the spare key hidden under the flowerpot and unlocked the door that evening to check on her friend, she found her still on the ground upstairs with half her face gone.

TREE

The maple having died years ago while a walnut
sprang up beside it, inches between them, now
covered in vines, its own life strangled, the whole
misshapen form leaning south—I could have
long ago taken care of the clump, but mornings
I study its decay, one limb stark against the sky.
How fitting to see its reaching, a reminder of how
we can't always order our lives. We can aim for
beauty, but a mess is what we get instead. Years
ago, a few paces away, a deer, I discovered, had
died near a fence row. Maybe brought down by
coyotes—I couldn't say—it was stripped clean
by the time I came upon it. Told to move its bones,
I saw no need. The sun bleached them, and they
lay where they fell, a marker of mystery, a holiness
I thought best not to disturb. I'm no longer certain
why one day arrives as opposed to another, why
one life continues and another concludes, years
apart, decades even. Not much seems seamless
but, instead, disjunctive, all the old narratives
scattered, scene after scene orphaned, distinctly
itself. Belief, long believed, finds a way to hold
almost anything together —barn and curve of road,
owl and aubade, horizon and mass grave—but
but maybe belief is a word with which we've
grown exhausted, defending what it overlooks
or has to let go of. When I moved to this land,
I justified the choice, in part, because of a beech,

maybe a century old, whose trunk, six feet wide,
extended upward twelve feet before branching
into two limbs, each at least three feet thick,
a miracle to behold, and I daily walked beneath
it, then wide around it, admiring its ancient life.
Its symmetry felt whole, and that it had survived
so long I took as a comfort until, five years later,
one limb came down in a storm with the other
soon to follow, leaving only the trunk. Entrusted
to me, my small window of time, the beech had
collapsed; and raised on Biblical cautions, on
signs found everywhere, it was impossible not
to read this turn of events as a personal rebuke.
Maybe time holds no awareness of someone like
me, a man who from my first awareness felt time
escaping me, diminishing exponentially, a student
of earth's simplest forms, moss, clover, stones,
wanting to hold each closer than my own breath.
The beech had simply reached its own conclusion.
Maybe the land had come to me because I might
mourn the loss as no one else would and go on
mourning all my years, however few I'm given.
Lately, I'm ashamed to admit I've grown tired
of almost every conversation. I no longer care
to prove a point, to convince another, to pose,
to reposition, to anticipate how to offer a response.
Vines grow. They consume a tree. It eventually
falls, becomes the earth again. Maybe someone
is there as witness, who loves language, who
tries to hold its presence in the world a while
longer. All we do is explain what we think we

understand, understanding little but the silence
a voice is subsumed by. A part of me wonders
if the tree is even real, if it's a supposition posed
for the purpose of thinking on a life's work, how
—before it has begun—it often falls of its own
weight, without a whisper, no one to listen anyway.

TAKING UP THE CAUSE OF ENDEARMENT

Not yet seventy years roaming the earth,
yet all my moments of astonishment, added
together, have become a kind of eternity.

I just want to be inside the story becoming
more and more of itself and me, a small
presence inside it, praising all its unfoldings.

One moment, if we listen closely, is talking
to all the others. Maybe it's a voice of endearment.
Or maybe every moment holds forth every other.

No one is never not present. They crowd in
upon us. All their words are woven into ours.
Wherever we turn, we look through their eyes.

Could we bear every dove we've ever known
sounding their five notes at the same time? Or
was each note a rapture not calling our names?

A NONSTATISTICAL ANALYSIS OF THE FUTILITY OF STATISTICAL ANALYSIS

IT'S 7:04 p.m. on Tuesday, May 30, and I'm about to enter Fenway Park for what will be my first ever major league baseball game, sponsored by several dozen companies I don't want to give the satisfaction of listing here. On Jersey Street, where people queue up and discuss whether their e-tickets are downloaded and whether they're on your phone or my phone and whether you're sure those are the right ones, various strategically-placed stands sell assorted savory junk foods—one advertises PEANUTS—PISTACHIOS—CASHEWS; another boasts ITALIAN SAUSAGE and ALL BEEF HOT DOGS; and one purports to offer something called MONSTAH BAGS.[1] All are overpriced the way only sports games' food can afford to be overpriced.

Tonight, the Boston Red Sox will be facing the Cincinnati Reds.[2] The Sox far outrank the Reds, so people are gearing up to be pumped, hyped, and generally pleased. The atmosphere is cheerfully optimistic. Accompanying me is my best friend and life partner, who I will hereby refer to as M____ (as a sort of John Barth-inspired gesture, as well as to protect his anonymity, but it's more for the Barthian thing if I'm being honest).

---

[1] There seems to be an all-caps theme. What probably happened here is that one stand decided to put their product names in all caps to make a statement, and then the others felt like if they didn't follow suit, they were making an implicit counter-statement about their own offerings not being exciting or vibrant or tasty enough to warrant full capitalization.

[2] It took a while for me to adjust to the confusion—"Reds," to me, sounds like an abbreviation of "Red Sox." I'd like to hereby propose that all Major League Baseball teams form a kind of UNish tribunal to compare names and ensure no two mascots are too similar.

My reasons for attending this game are twofold. The first is that M____ thought (and I agreed) that it would be a shame to live in Boston for two years—within walking distance of Fenway Park, no less—and never experience one of the most cherished Bostonian pastimes. The second is that I wanted to analyze just why it is that people enjoy watching professional sports and what (if any) crucial, fundamental defects make such enjoyment impossible for me.

And M____ is here to show me the ropes—he's somewhat of an expert, having played baseball in elementary school, where he "never hit a single ball." Luckily, the ability to hit balls is not a prerequisite for understanding baseball culture or the game's rules, which rules are shaping up to be so convoluted and decision-tree-like that I wonder whether baseball is too ambitious an entry point into the professional sports scene.[3]

I scan my ticket with some difficulty while a man I can only describe as a skinny Chris Farley tells me my phone is not angled correctly with respect to the scanner and where to move it so that my ticket will be validated with whatever the maximum efficiency is for someone as inadept at scanning baseball tickets as myself. Throughout this interaction, I experience a creeping paranoia, like I'm in danger of being found out. I don't know what they could even discover—I haven't stolen anything, and I'm not attempting to smuggle any illegal contraband (such as food that was purchased elsewhere for a reasonable retail price) into the stadium, but I feel like an infiltrator nonetheless. I wonder how many games I'd have to attend before this sense of impostordom would subside. Does

---

[3] For example, did you know that in baseball, something called a "square" is used for determining how strikes are counted? M____ describes the "square" as such: "Imagine, like, the prime area where the bat will hit the ball, right? Which is like right in front of the catcher. It's invisible. It doesn't physically exist. You just have to know where it is. If it's out of the square and you don't swing, then you get a 'ball.' At four 'balls,' you get to walk for free to the next base. But if it's out of the square and you *do* swing, you'll get a strike."

everyone else here also feel like a fraud or a mercenary, to some extent? I don't think so. I'll get more into why I don't think so later.

The indoor section of the stadium is gray and drab and has a vague fried scent that somehow doesn't resemble any fried food I'm familiar with, and I quickly realize that what I'm smelling is the fry itself. I'm currently wearing a single N95, but there are no other masks in sight, which to me indicates a widespread and generalized lack of concern for the potential future consequences of one's decisions. An ability to live in the moment, in other words. There's a certain at-ease-ness to sports fans that I simply don't possess— not in my everyday life, and not at even my loosest, which, to be fair, is probably most people's business casual. As we head outside to our seats, my frustration at not being able to achieve the level of Zen nonchalance this place embodies begins to mount.

Our seats are pretty good ones. They're slightly elevated and about ten degrees to the right of the batter so that the path of pitched balls is nearly perpendicular to us. The older fans seated at the end of our row stand up and awkwardly shuffle out without making eye contact, and I don't sense that they're in any way resentful about having to let us in. There's a stereotype about sports fans being angry and belligerent, but they seem friendly so far. The friendliness feels more like *indifferent* friendliness than true generosity, but perhaps there's no meaningful distinction.

Salesmen traverse the stadium's rows, hefting crates of various snacks and drinks over their heads, making a real show of it, as if it requires immense skill.[4] Concession offerings phase in and out of rotation, but they include lemonade, seltzer, Bud Light, pizza, popcorn, cotton candy, and pretzels. The vendors sort of purposefully meander, barking the name of whatever they're selling for those unable to read the huge printed capital letters on their

---

[4] And perhaps it does—there's certainly a degree of upper body strength necessary (or at the very least, there's a real talent to not letting excruciating bicep pain show on one's face).

crates.[5] A giant screen on the opposite side of the stadium alternately displays players' stats, close-up shots of the game, and baseball fast facts like what the difference between a curveball and a slider is, which difference I don't have time to note before the screen changes again. Whenever batters switch, music that sounds like something that would have been played at one of my high school dances blares over Fenway Park's speakers for just a few seconds at a time[6]—there's a persistent refusal to allow even a moment of the game to pass without some form of entertainment.

Sports fans adhere to a complex social code of clapping, sighing, booing, cheering, and "oh"-ing. We are presumably supposed to

---

[5] It's difficult to fully gauge the complex relationship concessions sellers have with sports fans. Before purchasing refreshments, fans tend to complain that the offerings are too expensive, probably as a kind of preemptive penance for the poor (albeit small-scale) financial decision they're about to make. People who aren't interested in buying seem apathetic—like they don't even notice the sellers—or mildly annoyed. Early on in the game, I witness a passive-aggressive exchange between one seltzer seller (a pudgy, East-Coast-cheery guy with a wrist tattoo displaying the years 2007, 2013, and 2018*) and the newly formed friend group of fans in the row in front of me, during which the fans hesitantly ask to purchase some seltzer, and the seller tells them he'll "be right back. Five minutes," and the guy in front of me and slightly off to the right, who is virtually physically indistinguishable from the seller save for the absent wrist tattoo, says, "I *bet* he'll be right back" in that way people do when they're sort of challenging someone to not live up to his promise, and the seller apparently hears this, because when he returns, he says, "Sorry. It took *seven* minutes." The buyers and seller seem to be on all right terms by the end of it, though, because the purchase still takes place, and the seller thanks the buyers graciously, and I'm left wondering what exactly the point of all that was.

*Later research informed me that these are the years the Sox won the World Series, and I can't help but note that the next number in the sequence should mathematically be 2022.

[6] At 8:24 p.m., M____ identified a song as Daft Punk's "One More Time," quipping, "How much money does Daft Punk make from baseball games?" A bit later, the stadium blasted "Party Rock Anthem" by LMFAO, which a decade ago was ubiquitous to the point of tedium. In other words, my initial sense of the music selections' early-2010s-high-school-dance vibe was pretty much spot on.

know when to do each one because the audience of 37,000 is completely synched. I'm always a second or two behind the curve, and I never quite know why I'm making any given noise, besides that everyone else is doing it. I'm also acutely aware of how many people are coughing. As a result of the mass cultural trauma of the past few years, I've developed a kind of cough echolocation by which I can precisely pinpoint how far away and in which direction the culprit is sitting. At 7:12 p.m., I upgrade my N95 mask. This new one is yellow and nerdy-looking and sticks directly to my face, ideally allowing no room for any unfiltered air to pass through. I put the old one back on top of it for good measure.

At 7:21, the first audience ball-catch occurs. The lucky fans are at about sixty degrees to the left of M____ and me and seem to be a family of about four. If it weren't for the giant net covering our own seats, M____ and my area would likely be a frequent target for stray balls (which, to be fair, is probably the same line of thinking the net-constructors had). According to M____, ball-catching is a significant facet of baseball culture. That's one thing I knew already, having read Don DeLillo's *Underworld* and being the annoying type who never misses an opportunity to mention it. I ask M____ whether seats are often chosen on the basis of ball-catching probability, and he doesn't know (all expertise must end *somewhere*, I suppose). Nonetheless, I find myself dully wishing we'd picked un-netted seats—catching a ball would make for a great story, and I could throw in some DeLillo allusions too. I suppose this will have to be good enough.

I might not be shaping up to have much in common with the fans, but here's something I share with a lot of the players: I'm left-handed. In the second inning, Boston plays four lefties in a row: Masataka Yoshida,[7] Jarren Duran, Enmanuel Valdez, and Reese

---

[7] who I must admit brought me a small amount of left-handed pride when he hit a double and scored a run in the ninth inning and was in large part responsible for Boston taking the game to a tight 9-8 Reds lead at the last minute, making

McGuire. They say left-handedness is often an advantage in professional sports because while left-handed players are accustomed to going against righties, the inverse is not true. When it seems like half of both teams are left-handed,[8] I'm not sure that logic holds.

Balls are tossed with an inhuman speed that simply has to be seen to be believed. They're more shot than thrown, fired like giant bullets across the entirety of the field in about as long as it takes to say, "whoa." They land neatly in catchers' mitts as if drawn there by some magnetic force or hurled down an invisible, turbo-charged zip-line.[9] Of the game's hundreds of throws, only one is dropped—by the Sox—and the outrage the folly produces makes me fear for the guy's safety. Much like the audience, their cheers and *ooh*s and

---

Boston's loss feel, if not quite triumphant, at least a bit less pathetic than it otherwise would have

[8] I later looked up the official statistic, and the left-handedness rate for professional baseball players is somewhere between 25 and 40 percent, which is not quite half but a noticeable jump from the 10-percent rate of the general population and probably explains why lefties seem so startlingly ubiquitous here.

[9] By the third inning or so, the catching thing seemed so practiced and frankly creepy that I began wondering how many baseball functions are dependent on catches' success—for example, does a dropped pitch by the catcher count as a strike? (I looked this one up later, and it turns out that there's an "uncaught third strike" rule with so many caveats and conditionals that it requires an entire Wikipedia page, and the rabbit hole runs deeper than I'm willing to delve in this essay. Nonetheless, if I were to ask anyone in the stadium about the rule, I have no doubt I'd receive a confident and accurate answer.* Point being, baseball is *complicated*, and baseball fans are perfectly willing to invest intellectual energy into understanding the nuances of something that matters to them.)

*And that's just basic, entry-level stuff—I haven't even gone into how many baseball fans dutifully retain hundreds of statistical datapoints: their teams' batting averages, seasonal hit and run (these verbs here being independent actions) numbers, batting averages against right-handed pitchers (because apparently the lefties throw off the data by a statistically significant amount), etc. It's not unlike my own childhood penchant for memorizing entire *Star Wars* visual dictionaries, complete with details on the size, speed, and make of ships that only appear for one shot in the entire saga, as well as comprehensive profiles of prequel characters who mostly just sit in the corner and nod contemplatively during official Jedi gatherings.

*ahh*s and *ohhhh . . . aw!s*[10] occurring in perfect harmony, the players apparently possess a hive mind. There's never any disagreement over who should retrieve a bat and to whom he should throw and which base's runner should be targeted, and I now consider the level of discipline and obsession that must be required to become part of a shared consciousness like this. Surely there isn't anything in my own psychic makeup that precludes me from reaching such state. And yet I never have. I have no clue what it would feel like to be positive that every person in your immediate vicinity knows your thoughts.

Sometimes mindreading isn't enough, however, and musings must be verbalized. People here talk continuously and loudly.[11] From what I can surmise, the most common topic of conversation is baseball—usually the current game, though sometimes earlier games are referenced, and often, general baseball theory is invoked. Here are some real quotes I heard during the first hour of the game:

"That *looked* like a strike, but it wasn't."

(In reference to the sound of a ball being solidly hit) "It's such a pleasant noise."

"As they make it to each base, they should have to kiss, fondle, and then have sex with the basemen. Don't you agree?" (No discernible response).

"Refs have to be really okay with being hit in the face. In ref practice I wonder if they say, 'Time to get hit in the face a few times. We need to destigmatize [*sic?*] it.'"

---

[10] This latter exhortation tends to happen when a bat looks like it will land fair, only to barely whirl out of bounds at the last possible moment.

[11] The decibel level is mostly a compensatory thing—they need to be heard over everyone else who is also talking loudly ("loudly" is an understatement; the default voice register here seems to be kind of a measured yell). Still, I wish it were somehow possible to break the feedback loop and lower the overall volume of the stadium by collective agreement—as it stands, this feels like a scenario in which raucousness can only ever intensify, and I can feel a headache developing.

"I'm gonna send that picture to my wife saying, 'We're hydrating with friends.'"

That last comment, made by the same man who earlier had the petulant stalemate with the vendor, was uttered right before taking a selfie of himself and the others in his row, their two-minute-overdue seltzers on proud display. What's worth noting is that none of these people knew each other when the game started. They all arrived separately and then somehow got intimately enough acquainted to want to be in a photo together. I've now been surrounded by thousands of people for over an hour and even forced to *interact* with some of them, and yet the only person I've actually spoken to is M____. This feels significant. The reason it feels significant is because M____ and I also have a full row of strangers surrounding us, and we have not even attempted to talk to them, nor they us, and there seems to be a kind of silent mutual agreement between us all that we aren't here to make friends with each other. This is a relief—I do not want to be their friend, and I feel strongly that they don't want to be mine. They'd probably be able to sniff out my impostor status from a mile away, so with only a few feet separating us, the stench must be overpowering. Besides, I just don't feel like we'd have anything in common.

But we do have at least one similarity: we all decided to attend this particular Red Sox game. Their reasons for attending might be vastly different from mine, but maybe they're not—the point is, I have no clue *what* their reasons are, because I can't get up the courage to start a conversation. I wouldn't even know what to say. Maybe something like, "Why are you here?" But that's the kind of question that seems to foretell its own answer and would likely only succeed at pissing them off.

If it seems like I'm making a lot of assumptions here, it's because I am. I guess that's another way I'm different from the others here—while I'm happy to let my brain run wild with hypotheticals, they're focused on what's in front of them. For the people in the row ahead of me, "what's in front of them" (or beside them, more accurately) are five other Red Sox fans whom they've never met before and might not ever speak to again but with whom they're still perfectly content striking up temporary, fleeting friendships. I've never had a single fleeting thing in my life.

These insights all occur during the seventh inning, while Cincinnati makes a run that brings the score to 4-0, and I observe with mild detachment that the existential dread exhibited by my fellow game attendees mirrors my own,[12] but I don't dwell on that similarity. Instead, I come up with more ways in which we differ. One obvious one is that these people, as evidenced by the widespread distress the Cincinnati lead is causing, are very invested in Boston winning. I, despite my red-and-navy V-neck advertising the Red Sox, do not particularly care. If pressed, I may even express a slight, negligible, deep-seated preference for the Reds, if only because their victory would be a lot more interesting from a journalistic analysis perspective. I briefly muse on whether this makes me some kind of low-level professional-sports psychopath.

Another difference is that baseball fans seem genuinely energized by crowds, while I am drained by them. Whenever the teams switch, the stadium's giant screen plays zoomed-in live-cam footage of audience members, and the camera victims all react the same way—first, they display the oblivious expressions of those who are unaware they're being filmed; next, one of them looks up at the screen and then briefly down again and then back up with the intensity of a dawning realization before hurriedly nudging the other implicated parties so that they can all whoop and wave. At

---

[12] Just for fun, here are a couple statements I overheard as Boston's situation began to look more dire:

"There he goes to second" (uttered with resigned observation while a Cincinnati player whose name I didn't quite catch did exactly that).

"This is worse than watching the races. This is terrible" (thus confirming one of my suspicions about fandom-overlap in the sports-viewing world).

one instance, the camera pans to a chubby kid of around ten, who is doing a kind of rotating-fists-plus-belly-roll dance move and maintains his cool even after noticing he's on the big screen. He receives a great collective laugh from the stadium, which I'm sure does wonders for his ego.[13]

At 8:44 p.m. I participate in a "wave."[14] This is a successful one—it travels around the entire stadium three times, and by the third, I'm wondering whether I've been trapped in a perma-wave reminiscent of the Nixonian seventies' descriptions of perma-trips, but it mercifully fizzles out after a particularly solid bat by Boston. Some people in the booth next to us try and fail to start their own wave and are subjected to light ridicule by some of the meaner fans.

At 8:58, Boston brings in a new pitcher, the left-handed Joely Rodríguez, whose introduction is a hype-inciting promo video in which he does the sign of the cross. The switch-out does seem to be a Hail Mary of sorts. Tack on an Our Father and it'll be like I'm right back in Catholic elementary school.

The religious nature of Rodríguez's video does raise some questions about the religious nature of baseball spectatorship in general, however. While this game is not quite like any other experience I've had, my most comparable point of reference is probably Catholic Mass.[15] The ritual aspect, the way everybody knows exactly

---

[13] In a later "dance-off" (aka, the ritual of showing fans onscreen while 2010s club music blares), the camera targets this same kid, who does a bit of a worse job hiding his excitement this time, and if that wasn't cruel enough, it comes back to him a *third* time, and by now he must be thinking *what are the chances?* and has a face-clasping, *Home-Alone*ish, seratonic meltdown right there on camera. This earns him more laughter from the crowd, as well as a fancy red "Dance-Off Champion" badge, which asserts itself across the bottom of the screen. If the game can be said to have any true MVP, it's probably this kid.

[14] in which people stand up and sit down and then the people on their immediate left stand up and sit down, creating a visual effect too self-explanatory to name again, with active participants often throwing up their arms and cheering, for maximum impact.

[15] whose hive mind I also never felt fully present in, it's worth noting.

what to do and when, the familiarity and predictability, the collective spirit that's greater than the sum of its parts…I could go on. In short, sports fandom is essentially secular church. If you don't believe me, try insulting your closest male relative's favorite team and watch as his face assumes the violated expression of a devout Christian at an occult-themed strip club.[16] A similar argument could be made for concerts—any gathering with like-minded people for the purpose of observing and occasionally participating in a spectacle falls into the category I have in mind (which, to avoid clunkiness, I'm going to refer to as Crowded Spectacle from now on).

On the level of Crowded Spectatorship, it's easy for me to connect with sports fans—I've been to many such events and even enjoyed some of them. However, I still can't help but point out that there's one obvious difference between sports matches and other Crowded Spectacles: competition. If you're devoutly religious and attend a church service, you're almost definitely going to come away feeling closer to your own personal conception of God, save for some acute spiritual crisis. If you see your favorite band in concert, you're pretty much banking on having a great time, or else you're asking for a refund. At a sports match, there's no such guarantee. The looming possibility that you'll have an awful time is what makes it *exciting* to fans. Enduring the depressing depths of watching your team get trounced only makes their eventual comeback (if it happens) feel more earned. This is not a feeling I can relate to. To me, it's a bit like buying concert tickets and not knowing whether they're for Radiohead or Imagine Dragons, or attending Mass and being told that today's reading will come from the Book of Satan.

---

[16] As we headed out for the night, M____ and I came up with a hushed but delightfully evil and for safety reasons purely theoretical variation on the Penis Game of our youth, in which one person whispers, "Go Cincinnati" and the other repeats it slightly louder, ad infinitum or ad- someone either fails to say the phrase at a higher volume than its last utterance or gets beat up by angry baseball fans.

But despite the unpredictability of live professional baseball being the whole fun of it, baseball cataloguers crunch serious numbers keeping careful record of teams' wins and losses and players' individual profiles, helping to ensure that game outcomes are, in theory, incredibly predictable. And yet, their predictions still aren't perfect. For example, the Red Sox *should* be winning tonight, but after a grand slam in the seventh inning that brings the score up to 8-0 Cincinnati, that result is looking increasingly less likely, and spectators are beginning to react the way you might expect Radiohead fans who have unexpectedly found themselves at an Imagine Dragons concert to react. I fear that petty crimes of passion may soon be afoot in Fenway.

At 9:26 p.m., it's time for us all to sing an off-tune rendition of "Take Me Out to the Ball Game," a longstanding baseball tradition, according to M____. The screen displays tonight's accompanist: an older man crouched over an electric piano that's dialed to a kind of eerie Depeche-Modeish preset. The man has the posture of someone who has spent decades playing organs at church services. The audience stands for the song, and I nearly place my right hand over my heart, likely because I've subconsciously noted the commonalities between various spectator singing rituals. I sing like the best of them. I might be an impostor, but if you saw me now, you'd never know it. I even experience one moment of brief elation—a sliver of what I assume sports fans must feel for entire games[17]—followed by an intense wave of internal backlash for allowing myself to feel it. I've done nothing to earn it.

And then I ask myself why my contentment needs to feel "earned." Is this the true difference between them and me?[18] And

---

[17] It is, of course, worth noting that the catalyst for my fleeting good spirits is the dramatically ironic dread with which the crowd sings the lines, "*Let's root, root, root for the home team/If they don't win, it's a shame.*"

[18] But, like I said earlier, they also have this need. They earn joy by watching their team do well, whereas I earn it by....Well, the jury's still out, I guess.

isn't there a kind of sick solipsism implicit in my whole endeavor? For the past three hours, I've been operating under the assumption that I possess some unalterable psychic anomaly that can be objectively analyzed and quantified instead of admitting that I actively and deliberately position myself against an amorphous social mass whom I have no real desire to get to know and that I make willful and calculated efforts to poison potentially worthwhile experiences by doing things like bringing notepads to organized sporting events on which to make lists of all the reasons I don't enjoy organized sports. I, in short, am addicted to isolation. And my addiction has only grown more insatiable over the past few years, during which I've had an actual *excuse* for not forging transient yet meaningful connections with others or even maintaining the long-term connections I already had. Maybe I don't just dislike unpredictability but actually *fear* it. Maybe I'll never properly join polite society for the same reason I'll never enjoy a baseball game— it's impossible to know what will happen. Social participation is an experiment wherein others are dependent variables swirling around in a giant interactive communal soup, bumping into each other and affecting each other and changing the trajectory of each other's lives in ways that can never be foreseen or statistically measured. The same unpredictability that's invigorating for some is, to me, a nightmare scenario reminiscent of the one happening in Fenway Park right now as thousands of Red Sox fans grapple with the reality that the Red Sox are going to lose a baseball game they should, by all estimates, be winning.

But they'll get over it. They'll live. Maybe I will too.

IN PRAISE OF RANDOM THINGS, JUNE 21ST

Praise for the light—its certainty, the way it fractures
into geometric patterns I see tracing
on the sidewalk, the way it clings to the wings of birds

Praise for Zoom—the way the early morning visit
with my Israeli grandson sketches missing pieces in my family portrait
like stick figures trying their best to become real.

For the waffle sandwich—gobs of blueberries and strawberries
stuffed between two Belgians and topped with more whipped cream
than the Himalayas have snow

For the house wren riot—and the way the ruby-throated packet of
hyper-caffeinated energy sipped my sugar syrup for 6 nanoseconds
before flitting away

Blessing for little blonde boy—holding his nylon shorts away
from his sides like a blue sail lifting in the wind,
running and laughing the whole way down my block

Rise up in praise for the Amazon rep— who did not disconnect me,
disrespect me, disapprove
or disappoint me

Praise for Wordle— in two moves

For chord progressions—the skeletons of songs rattling their
twelve- bar bluesy bones in my Air Pods,
accompaniment for my walking pulse

And the lone doe—the way she tiptoes in the whisper music
of grass just at dusk and delicately nibbles
my neighbor's fallen fruit instead of my flowers and shrubs

Praise for your good night kiss—4 hugs in held suspension, books
on my night table, the entirely of them, bread dough that did not fail
to rise, 60 ounces of water, indoor plumbing

This good hair day— dark chocolate and coffee, coffee and
dark chocolate, for the completely possible poem,
the smile on my friend's face when we met for lunch

For the chipmunk so quick I did not run it over— and the light,
the way the lemon bash of it
drops at day's end like a scene change in the theater

FOR MY LOVE ON HIS 80TH BIRTHDAY

Let us not repeat the lies
told by numbers,
make jokes about forgetting words
or say if our faces slip
in the fogged bathroom mirror
if we can touch our toes quick
and supple like a robin landing.

Let us not make mention
of how things have come untied
like shoelaces
or what we used to be good at
and now are no good at all.

Let us not rehash
how quickly noon became night
or what's whispered to us at 2 AM:
what we've done and left
undone, mortal boundaries
or the possible natures of time

Instead, let's do this:
start by saying aloud one moment
larger now: like how it is when we glide
in on our bikes, the beautiful miles
traveled yet again

or the other day,
walking in the Gardens
and spotting the Twilight Zone roses
pulsing off their stems,
fruity purple growing
louder and louder

or just now
when I whispered
I'll always love you
three times in a row,
not the words meandered and multiplied
but the low untranslatable song
of things folded between us
and our laughter
like the sound of many rivers.

TREE MEN

YOU'RE as likely to be hit twice by lightning on a Monday as see a wood-chipper pull a man into its maw. Rare, as well, is the member of an arborist crew who hasn't witnessed the horror from the safety of his imagination. Such was I that season, a clinically depressed college boy on medical leave from my nervous scholar's struggle. I took a job with the Walters Tree Service in Winchester, Virginia, hoping outdoor work would be the answer where titrations of the calming pharmacopeia had failed, as if manual labor wasn't host to its own spectrum of anxiety. My parents, unaware of the depth of my depression, hoped I might study a foreign language in the interim, against a permanent divorce from academia. My girlfriend, whom I supposed found nothing to admire in a man who'd spend a year cutting trees rather than tasting the culture of a European capital, ghosted me before the term became fashionable.

Mr. Walters, who hired me, asked if I was afraid of heights? At my hesitance he told me not to worry. "You won't be climbing, just feeding the chipper. Why do you want this job anyway? Let's see your hands….roll up your sleeves." Only later, I realized that my greatest fears were of things I'd never reached for, and that my girlfriend's estrangement had more to do with intimacy I hadn't dared than any lack of ambition.

I'd been cutting cord wood for my family's fireplace for years, and passed Mr. Walters' physical with no trouble. It was the college-boy thing and untamed hair that gave him doubts. I said I'd 'always been interested in…' "Stop," he threw up his hands. "I don't need a tree-hugger. I'm clearing off trouble. I don't care if you know sumac from a locust shoot." I began to explain myself, but he interrupted again. "Where do you live? No drugs? Living at home, are you? Assume you can drive?"

"This is your new man," he told the crew boss Vernel, whose jaw fell at the sight of me. "No stranger to hard work," Walters said, pulling this bogus resume out of the blue. In fact, I was a complete stranger to physical labor as daily duty. An ordinary middle-class son of America, my exposure to the liberal arts curriculum had taught me my forebears were canny as any in labor saving devices, starting with slavery, moving on to factory children, then machinery, and a myriad of outdoor machines like Mr. Walters' second-hand chuck-and-duck wood chipper which lacked safety features.

At the time, his crew was working on private land, taking down dead ash trees. In an open field they needed no preliminary topping. The trunks and larger limbs were being cut for firewood, the smaller fed to the chipper. Right away I was shown how to throw the butt-end of branches with force at the noisy machine's mouth, then step back and wait for the lower masticating whine as chips showered into the hopper behind. Nothing but the short entry chute between me and the machine's rolling teeth. If it could chew up a six-inch log, imagine how easily it could digest me. "Do what he tells you," Walters said, pointing at Vernel, whose shrug made his disapproval clear. In the crew's new pecking order I'd be pecking last, and I was content with that. It was what I'd wanted, just to be ordered here and there with months of mental vacation ahead. But there was no clean-scrub of the student brain. Outdoor work could not free me from classrooms where I still walked in academic nightmares.

You might ask, 'If dreams are the work of mad authors and absent editors—fantasies arriving uninvited—why reproduce them here?' Because in this early stage of my time among the arborists, unsettling dreams and daydreams were central to the experience, one of them as tormenting in slumber as it was inane on waking. I was protesting a history exam written in ideograph. Bewildered, I was asked by the professor if I'd been absent the day the class learned Chinese.

As academic anxiety gradually gave way to the dangers of my new occupation, there came a particular night of horror when I saw the fingers of a severed hand balanced atop the gate of our wood-chip hopper, as if one of the crew was trying to climb out. Impossible, because I'd just seen him pulled off his feet, arms and head first, surrendering at the same pace as an ash branch to the machine's mechanical appetite. It was turning him into a crimson coloration in the top layer of chips. The crew chief Vernel was grinning at me as a dangling foot disappeared. Then I was trying to explain the impossibility of a casket funeral to the man's mother.

Three of my five crew mates were authentic wage laborers, I supposed as far into the future as their imaginations carried them; their lives seemed as settled as the brands on their beer cans. What regard should they have for an interloper from a world where thinking was considered work? They never sent me to Home Depot for sky hooks or black-and-white-striped paint, but kept me at a third-person distance while I was no threat to their ranking.

No welcome for me in crew-chief Vernel's cold, gray eyes set in inward contemplation, promising no hope of brotherhood. He might have been speaking to someone behind him, explaining how far he'd come to sit on his top rung. At his direction I kept ice in the water bucket, put the traffic cones out and at times held a stop sign.

After a month I was still not trusted with a chain saw. I felt no resentment, rather wondered at the contentment of others, at ease with their weekly paychecks and tins of tobacco. There was Ron who dipped RedMan and hummed through the day, giving rhythm without melody to the day's back-and-forth; Gene who preferred Skoal, and would flummox me with sexual inference or a question for which there was no self-respecting response; "A good day's work and a piece of pussy 'd probably kill him." or "Still using your hand?" If I parried, "get a life," it only begged his question and kept me subject to the crew's amusement.

Then Jefferson, mute until spoken to, the one who might have accepted me as a deserving workmate if I had only paid full dues of a new man. Vernel was the only one whose soul seemed as calloused as his hands. When we were especially busy an extra man might be hired from the end of the walking mall where leftovers of Winchester's wasteland of alcohol and opioid addiction waited each morning looking for day labor.

The crew kept me aware of my schooling, both how much and how little it meant in their estimation of me. If I'd lived in class-rooms all my life, how unlikely I could learn anything from life itself. How useless to know that every action has an equal and opposite reaction if I was going to fall back on my ass the first time I threw a heavy limb at the chipper. I tried not to let some line of poetry, or a statesman's quotation betray me, or any showy knowledge that might cause an eye-roll or a spurt of tobacco juice.

I've omitted our climber Carl from the list — a man apart, who made a remarkable twenty dollars an hour with the right to hire out on weekends. The climber is the acknowledged hero of a small tree company like Walters'. Working without a bucket-truck's perch of relative safety, he may climb on spiked boots a hundred feet or more, with his carabiners, and ropes and D rings to hang over the earthbound in his belted saddle. Swinging by lanyard or high-hung safety line, he hops limb to limb, sometimes tree to tree, an arbor jockey, operating his hip-hung chainsaw one handed, appearing fearless on branches that can scarcely support him.

How fragile his small fame. Not long after I arrived Carl broke his back, falling in a giant oak. Hanging limp on a life-saving branch of the last tree he'd ever climb, we might have thought him unconscious or dead but for an intermittent howl of pain. Gene made a shaky ascent with Vernel calling up instructions, muttering "should have gone up there myself." He was offering instruction for maneuvers already accomplished when Carl was secured in a rope harness and lowered to the ground where the EMTs were waiting. I was grateful to be one of the earthbound. Not long afterward I was high in the branches of a tree I couldn't remember climbing, falling backward, before I came crashing down on my mattress.

The crew's politics reached scarcely beyond their own welfare. To take gloom off the day of the accident, Mr. Walters had treated us all to lunch at Knosos, the Greek franchise in Winchester. Here I was pushed to the front as the one who would know what spanakopita was. Facing a swarthy man serving behind the counter with a hand wrapped in gauze, I asked what had happened to him.

"Burned," he said.

"Grease?"

"No, Pakistan."

Turning to share my amusement with the others I saw not a grin among them, only grim nodding at a mutual sense of betrayal by the country's misguided angels of immigration. Not one of them thought the government owed them a thing. No more did I. None ready to accept a favor gracefully, unwilling to be beholden.

Carl got severance; his life in Virginia's green canopy was over. Lost to the crew was his tree craft, source of their pride and proxy dominion over tall trees. There were thousands of crews like ours across a whole continent of dying ash and other problem trees, crews with their own climbing heroes. But to hear Vernel tell it, one might have thought Carl's leverage from the top of a giant oak could move the planet. I wondered if our little company would survive his loss while the new fear took its place in my library of dreams.

WE were all laid off for a week after Carl's fall while Mr. Walters searched the region for his next climber. A scribbled resume insufficient; Walters wanted to see a new man's skills for himself. He found him working high over an estate by the Potomac River. Hired him right out of a tree at a salary known only to him and Mr. Walters. The man showed up the next week in a rusty truck with his gear thrown in the back. Hitching himself up in his straps he looked us over, appraising the crew one by one.

HIS name was Jasper Embry. His red face was pitted, perhaps from smallpox or severe acne. Behind hawkish features his steady gaze revealed nothing. His black hair pulled back in a knot left clear view of a growth on his temple, a dark nickel-size disk. With his narrow jockey's body, shirt buttoned to the neck, and sweat-darkened leather pants he looked all country without apology.

"From below Grinders," Embry said, "a ways off in the mountains."

One imagined a few bungalows on a blue highway whose event might be a crossroad, and infrastructure, a speed trap. Walters told us Embry had spent twenty-three years in trees and didn't need a leaf- identification book or bark-chart to tell one tree from another. As if to say his work had taught him how to do it, and approaching a tree he did not mean to hug it, but to rid the world of another nuisance.

Embry was already studying his first climb, a double-trunk maple, the larger half split by lightning. Its top branches, brittle by nature, were hanging over a greenhouse.

"You have insurance yet?" Vernel asked him.

"He'll be my ground-man."

I stepped back because Embry was pointing at me.

"He just chucks," Vernel told him.

"I'll have him anyway," Embry said, maybe because I was the fresh-faced one, and moving backward as others came forward for preferment. Vernel pointed at Ron.

"No, I'll have him." Our new climber was still pointing at me.

There could be no shrinking out of sight. Vernel looked to Walters for support, but got none. He may have been in charge of ground men, but Mr. Walters wasn't crossing his new hire. When the boss was gone Vernel pulled the others aside. They were all looking at me.

From that day forward I was Embry's aide, though still Vernel's minion. First thing, the new climber taught me the cow-hitch. He had me tie one around the bottom of a nearby mulberry, setting up the control line that would carry branches safely over the greenhouse. There was snickering as I fumbled through my first lesson.

Walters had been wrong about Embry. He leaned against the maple, feeling its scarred bark in a kind of apologetic salute. On that first day, watching his smooth ascent, his easy movement, branch to branch, my interest in the work woke up. Agile, as if sprung by steel sinew, alert as a squirrel, he rose like an anti-gravity machine, his feet gripping the bark like the hooked side of velcro. Forgetting my fear for the moment, I could imagine myself his pupil.

Somewhere up there, out of sight, a thrush or its winged cousin began to trill and warble, maybe in surprise at human company. Then other birdsong as if the first had attracted competition. Embry pulled up the chainsaw hanging from his belt, gave the starter cord a single tug. A moment later a limb was swinging from a rope as if a baton was demanding more chirp and trill. I realized it wasn't birds at all. It was Embry himself producing the chorus. From some magic of breath, tongue and lips, he was making a music of grace-note speed, more like a gift of nature, than anything that could be taught or learned.

The branch-walking that followed had the weightless appearance of a marionette as he tied off limbs, sawed, and released them to be safely lowered over the greenhouse. Chainsaw, birdsong, chainsaw, and birdsong again. Watching and listening, the men below looked up slack-jawed, ignoring the pile of branches growing beside us. Vernel got out of the truck where he'd been pouting. "Walters ain't paying him to whistle," he said, insulted by the music. He said no one could equal Carl in a tree, and the crew went back to work as Embry flew to the damaged side of the maple.

WITHIN a week I had mastered our new climber's instruction in several knots—running bowline, alpine butterfly, and prusik hitch, the loop that that holds fast on the middle of a line. Before long I was helping prepare his ropes as he studied the next ascent. Vernel had been watching me as a road-gang guard might a convict testing the range of his shotgun. He made sure I was busy with the two-fingered signal that meant his eyes were on me. When I wasn't helping Embry I was chucking branches, raking twigs, or on the road holding the stop sign. After a few weeks Embry told me, "You can call me Jasper, young fella." A heady promotion. As our bond grew, he hired me to work with him on weekends beyond the crew's notice. By then he felt free to ask me why I didn't get off my ass and move out of my parents' house. Hadn't finished college yet, I told him.

On an otherwise dismal day, hearing his aviary singing, I could call up to him some line of pastoral poetry, without fear of laughter. "What's it like at that place" he asked me later, "just thinking all day long?"

Vernel was calling Embry "Feathers." I hoped for a counter-attack, but none came, the disrespect clear enough but Embry ignored it. When Walters called me into his office, I knew something was off, and thought he might be getting rid of me. He asked what was going on. He said Vernel had told him I wasn't much account, and what did I have to say for myself. "Did you get off on the wrong foot?"

"There isn't any right foot with him," I told him, and was surprised when he said, "Maybe there isn't. If you stay another few months I'll raise you to eight dollars. Just do what he tells you for now." He wanted to know if the state inspector had been around, and if Vernel was doing side work on the company clock.

He was showing me out the door, ignoring my protest at being used as a spy.

I told Walters I'd work another few months if he wanted me, though I'd be ignoring the deadline for readmission to college, passing on scholarship money, and triggering my parents' eviction notice. The truth is I was more afraid of going back to college—maybe total immolation in that mental furnace—than facing whatever Vernel might have in store. By then I was in full sway of my 'country uncle' Jasper Embry and his daily example. I wanted more than his tutoring and tolerance; I wanted his admiration. Not possible while I was content to handle ground ropes, sharpen his chains and keep his saws topped up with gas and chain-oil. Reading my mind, he said, "I could run that fear out of you."

I TOOK two rooms over an antique store in Winchester's walking mall. A few weeks went by before I dared ask Jasper up to my new quarters for a beer, perhaps a step too far, reaching for premature brotherhood. I was more apprehensive than gratified when he said, "OK, young fella," and showed up a few nights later.

"It's all right," he said, but looking over the bed and chair in the otherwise bare rooms I knew he meant we should walk out to a bar for our beer. Maybe he thought he'd insulted me because in the bar he began to share a story beyond my asking.

I'd been wrong about the little community he'd come from. Not three houses on a blue highway; far more remote. A few cabins deep in the West Virginia mountains, farther than you could see across the rolling landscape from the Interstate. On a logging road beyond state maintenance. Each home, a fortress with a hound on a chain. "Too low in the hollow for rabbit ears to catch the television," they made their own entertainment, he said. Burlap dolls, and a rocking horse from a pallet. They lived what people in the city called the folk-life. He knew this because his father had been taken to Washington one summer where a fuss was made over his carving and he showed how he fashioned his walking sticks. They had one there in a museum in a glass case.

Think of four families, bound by the necessities of survival, but separated by pride of tribe, and two children in forbidden alliance. Thurjean at fifteen in Jasper's arms defying her father who had warned Jasper's: "Keep your bastard away from my daughter." One night she put fireflies in a glass tube and rolled it up in her straw-blond hair. Jasper thought he was "in heaven dancing with an angel." When they were old enough to run over the mountain without getting caught, he carried her off to Winchester where he started in tree work. Thurjean studied house-keeping on-the-job, and the science of not having babies. As Jasper's work grew into a career, she managed the money and did the book-keeping.

"Right away, so happy." A real life folk-tale, I thought. The boy with the scarred face and knot on his head whistling up a princess.

"In the stories," Jasper asked me, "don't the trials come first, then the princess?"

As the sun fell Jasper stared in disgust at a wasted day. We were meant to take out two dead oak trees together but that Saturday morning was frozen. "If your fingers go numb, you won't know if you cut one off or just mashed it." We sat in his truck through the middle of the day while it poured icy rain. He knew a man who had worse luck than Carl; "slid out of a sycamore in a rain like this and broke his neck." The wind blew a gale through the afternoon til it was "too late to make a showing." We drove back to the Winchester bar where he'd begun telling his story. Now he wanted mine.

"Where'd it go wrong for you, young fella?"

I explained how a doctor had said my brain got too busy to live with itself.

That can happen to anyone, he said. He knew of a man whose "head got so stuck on one of those twisty blocks they had to send him to the fifth floor," the locked ward of the Winchester hospital.

"That boy wasn't right," he said, "but look at you."

53

What did he mean?

"Running backward. Spooked by the books. Now you're too scared to climb a tree. Do you want to top out like Vernel? Be ground boss of tree beetles all your life?" Looking up at him every day was just teasing my fear, he said.

The next weekend he said we had a job in West Virginia. On the way he could see I didn't believe him. I was nervous.

"Guess you didn't know I worked way back on a crew with Vernel."

How would I know if he'd never told me?

"A man got struck with a falling branch, and Vernel threw the blame on me. We was both fired. It's no secret. He's told Walters his side of it."

We reached a farm road and Jasper drove across to the fence line, stopping under a tall poplar.

"You've been watching how for months," he said.

If I wasn't frightened before, by the time he'd put me in his spurs and saddle I was shaking like another poplar leaf. Hardly in control of arms and legs as he talked me up to the first low perch. Unrelenting, he told me, hand by hand, how to put slack in the safety lanyard. "Now pick up your feet." I was hanging by the climbing rope. The shaking stopped. When I put a foot down again I was standing light as an astronaut on the moon, then stepping softly out the branch and back again.

On the ground again, I was giddy.

That was a start, he said.

Jasper took me out to the same tree several times in the next weeks, each time coaxing me higher until I'd reached the canopy with a chain saw hanging from my hip, working in the highest branches. No more involuntary shakes.

With my progress I presumed a full brotherhood, and without invitation I drove out to find Jasper's house where Winchester bumps up against the countryside. The fancier homes to either side of his little place were built on higher ground. The small home looked like a squatter that had defied the bulldozers as 'colonials' gathered around to shame it. His gravel drive went down a short incline to an entrance on a gable end. Paint was peeling, glazing all crackle, and the screen door hanging crooked in its jamb.

No greeting but "What are you doing here?"

It took him a while to come to the door, but through the screen I could see a floor plan he might have brought with him from the mountains—kitchen, dining and bedroom all one. Bed covers thrown aside, a scatter of dishes and dirty laundry, and no sign of a princess. Leading me back to my car, he had nothing to say.

Back with the crew the next week I tried to apologize to him. He waved it off with the back of his hand. "She run off two months ago," he said.

"Thurjean?

"No, Thurjean was way back." He'd had two women since then. This last one had cleared out overnight, another woman, he explained, who had lost patience with her fate, and then with a neighbor's assistance, discovered she'd been a "victim of mental abuse." Before she left, she emptied his bank account. Took the dog too. She hadn't got far, he guessed, because the dog had found its way home again.

JEFFERSON was first to be fired. The others looked at me balefully. Wasn't I to blame for being there at all. There was a tacit competition after that, all vying to be judged indispensable, but unsure who they were trying to impress, Jasper or Vernel, who thought he was about to be fired himself. That's when he started referring to Jasper as "that gravel-faced bastard" instead of "Feathers." Jasper was still turning his back on the abuse. I supposed his silence was a gathering storm. I was waiting for thunder.

Walters called me up to say I'd be going back to college soon. If so, he knew more than I did, or maybe it was his way of letting me go. "You may be clever," he said, "but you're ignorant. Working for him you could both be sued. Tell him I want to talk to him."

"Why don't you tell him yourself," I said, waiting to be fired. There was an audible breath and a sighing exhale before he said, "His phone's been cut off."

That was a Sunday evening. The crew worked through the next week, ears cocked for the sound of Walters' diesel, lest one of them be caught idling. They were waiting for another shoe to fall. Then another week and they were back to normal, taking turns napping in the truck, thinking trouble must have blown past. But Friday morning I was walking by Vernel with an armful of sumac shoots when he pushed himself into my load. I tripped and fell to the ground. Jasper from his high perch came flying down his climbing line to see why all the men were standing over me. Vernel was giving me a hand up as if nothing had happened.

At quitting time Vernel climbed out of the truck where he'd been dozing. He came over to join the others, showing late-in-the-day solidarity with men who took his orders. We were standing there watching him toss a last locust branch at the chipper. He was still pointing at the roaring machine when his sweater snagged on a thorn and began to unspool in dancing circles from his wrist. As the red line travelled out, the sleeve was disappearing up to his elbow and beyond, the flying line circling past his bicep in frightening surrender, unraveling backward through the order of its knitting. With the denuding of his arm, and all the yelling lost in the chipper's clamor, eternity collapsed into the moment the line snapped free of his shoulder.

WITH the motor silenced, Vernel stood there still pointing at the defeated machine. Then turned to look at me, posing like a death-defying magician, satisfied his trick had worked to perfection. Jasper was pulling me away, telling me, "That man is dangerous. You can't work here anymore." The others were standing beside Vernel, watching my retreat. I told Jasper I'd already been fired. I'd be coming back Monday for my last paycheck. That I held no grudge against any of them. They had every right to resent me and my disruption, knowing I'd be going back to that place where states of concentration were considered work.

MONDAY had broken gray over the farm where the crew waited to say a false farewell to the college boy. Jasper never came down from his high seat in the oak whose dead limbs threatened the house below. He had his own way of saying goodbye. Secure above an ill-natured world, above men whose kindest regard was an admiring envy, above his home over the horizon that could not hold a woman, over the lines of a pitiless phone company, above the boy who proved not worth the trouble he'd spent on his climbing education; still offering grace notes against earthbound disappoint-ment; superior in aerial skill and song. Not one bird and then another, but a medley of trill and warble I hadn't heard before, as if springing unrehearsed from some ancestral habit of questing or contentment, the source maybe a secret from himself. Flying through leaves to his next perch.

Not caring what others thought of me, I raised my voice to Jasper, "So little cause for caroling of such ecstatic sound, written on the world below, both near and far around." Getting it all wrong, but not what most needed saying: "some hope whereof he knew, and I was unaware."

CASSANDRA

At recess, the boys pinched her budding breasts.
She cried but didn't flinch. The mean girls laughed.
The teachers ignored her honest protests.
As if by divine will, a turgid shaft
of sunlight penetrated a cleft cloud.
Just one teacher (the faculty short-staffed)
helped her stand and shooed away a thick crowd
of children abuzz with rumor. The nurse
took note of the bruises. Behind the shroud
of office walls, the principal was terse,
rebuking. Her father threatened to sue.
At last, beaten, all he could do was curse
the Church. His daughter learned what was her due:
Her witness would be mistrusted, and true.

PRIAM

"What of it? Priam dies. All fathers die.
"As do all good sons." She traced the outline
Of his face, the full lips, the aquiline
Nose, heavy brows that framed each almond eye.
She marked the dead body. "We must comply
"With heaven's mandate. This ravished rough shrine
"Betwixt my legs, where this king drank his wine,
"And reveled . . . my God, is no longer mine.
"An apostate will lie in this royal hall
"And spill his seed upon the sacred stage."
Now she caressed her own face, the swart mien.
She gouged her fingernails, as if to scrawl
Prophecy on her cheeks: "Here died a queen."
Her dry breasts would nurse her hate and her rage.

MY GREEN JOB

I stumbled into it. My sister's friend had been dating this environmental engineer who needed somebody part-time, and I needed something part-time, so I said, *What the hell?*

This was late in 1991, and Pierrette and I and baby Emily had just moved to Spokane. So I paid the guy a visit—I flew the green flag when I could, though I wasn't all that sure what Environmental Engineers actually *did*. Did they carve meanders back into the courses of rivers? Could they plant the gaping grave of a pit mine with roses and daisies? And then the guy started talking about marketing, and I said to myself, well, maybe with some judicious wriggling, I could handle marketing.

When I mentioned I'd done a bit of writing, the conversation turned, and after a while the guy—the Guy—told me of his urgent need for someone to go off to the Spokane Public Library to look up historical data about a certain property. And to maybe write the historical data into a report? And maybe also write up the notes provided by the Site Visitor, Doug, who had actually, physically, been there on the property?

CARTOPHILIA

And so it began, my job with the Guy Group. The Guy was innovative. He once explored the idea of purchasing a rock band's fog machine for indoor air circulation investigations. Now he was paying me to go to the library. Well, the library and other places, to look at maps and stuff.

The first map I gave serious attention to at the Library was in the 1934 Metsker's Atlas of Yakima County, a map for—what was it? —the Blodgett Property? The Blodgett Property on the Yakima River, where the wheat fields fringe into apple-and-wine country, now. I was told we were doing a Phase I Environmental Site Assessment—an ESA—and we were supposed to determine the earliest developed use of this property. My job was to look at records, and document my looking.

So I looked, and saw no signs of development, and I wrote that down. And since the Site Visitor had looked at the property, too, and had found no evidence of an Environmental Liability, we could then say we'd done our Due Diligence on behalf of the Client. I couldn't help but notice, though, that the patchworked properties on the Map were marked with interesting names: Leonard Funch . . . Clay Barn . . . Gaylord Freepons . . . Fidel E. Nunez . . . Billy Gene Phelps . . . Manly Shook . . . Benny Rocha . . .

Round, ripe seedful names such as these are seldom found and cannot be invented. So wrote William Gass about the names he once collected in the hope that *stories would suddenly shower out like dimes.*

Sounded good. And I started collecting names, writing them down in the back of my work notebook, a classic Elan E64 Field Book, water resistant, easy to carry, and with a High Visibility Orange cover. This became a pattern: I'd jot down my job data in the front of the Elan—the first of many Elans—and in the back I'd make notes about whatever else I felt like making notes about. Not so many stories showered forth, but the names had been there on the map: Guen Hermance . . . Harriet Hosko . . . Harland Knight . . . Wyatt Cone . . . Leonard Goodnight . . . And across the river rose the Horse Heaven Hills.

GRAPHOPHILIA

I had this tendency to write things. Once, during my single days, right before a young woman I was wooing left for a vacation in Oregon, I gave her a care package, a little paper sack of fortune cookies. Beforehand, I'd carefully tweezered the original fortunes out of their crispy shells and replaced them with limericks of my own device, these wry little poems all about her. I know I wrote at least five limericks, but could I have written as many as ten? I don't think so, but I was obsessive about things like that in those days. In any event, I was pretty well pleased with the project, though it didn't do the trick, wooing-wise.

When I started courting Pierrette, writing had become more of an early move than a last resort. We hadn't known each other long when I offered her one of my moderately published writings, a semi-polished semiprecious pebble, maybe in the way a stray cat tries to charm a favored human with the gift of a dead mouse. And maybe it worked—or maybe it was the pasta with walnut sauce. Or the white chocolate brownies.

I made a little—very little—money with some of my early writings, with essays about Ireland, about childhood games, about the weather in Seattle. I wrote a pamphlet advertising a Death Penalty Seminar for defense attorneys. Another time I worked on another pamphlet, a user's guide for an add-a-pearl necklace kit starring Freshwater Baroques.

And then writing helped me score my Green Job.

TAG TEAM

Pierrette and I had been aiming for part-time work so we could do split-shifts, tag team parenting. And it worked. Pierrette was with the kids, Emily, and soon enough Julia, in the morning, while I was doing my research for the Guy Group, and she did her physical therapist work in the afternoon when I was with the kids.

I changed thousands of diapers, made thousands of kid meals. Sometimes I had to improvise. One day when they wanted me to make pancakes, I had to hustle to the bookshelf and come back to the kitchen with a finger marking the spot where Nick Adams makes breakfast in Hemingway's "Big Two-Hearted River." I mixed and poured the batter and glanced at the story and compared what was happening in my skillet with what was happening in Nick's, the way the edges of his "cake began to firm, then brown,

then crisp. The surface was bubbling slowly to porousness." When
Nick shook his skillet and flipped his cake, I did the same with mine

WORKING FOR A LIVING

On another day, Emily came home with a question. Maybe
they'd been talking careers in second grade, but she'd been thinking.
She was concerned:

"Dad?"

"Hmm?"

"What did you grow up to be?"

Someone who looks up stuff for the Guy. And puts the stuff
into reports.

I'd never been a professional. I'd attended the University of
Montana, and had earned a bunch more credits than I needed to
graduate, but those credits were far too whimsically arranged to add
up to anything. So, making an actual living turned out to be tricky,
but by the time I started at the Guy Group, I'd pretty much settled
into office work. I could process words. I could enter data. I could
whip out a clean, precise business letter, stern or ingratiating, as the
case required. I was a known File Diver and General Purpose
Cratchit. An Administrative Assistant. Once, an Operations
Liasson Auditor. At least, that's what one particular boss and I
decided would look good on my résumé, on my last day on that job.

OR LOGOPHILIA

I worked for the Guy Group for quite a while. I dove into
writing and re-writing the Environmental Site Assessment reports
that crossed my desk, tweaking and tuning and streamlining.

Because why not say, "It was flat around there," rather than, as
one of my colleagues wrote, "The topography of the immediate
vicinity of the subject property was physically observed to appear
generally flat and level?"

And there had to be a cleaner way of explaining why the report needed historical stuff than, "The objective of reviewing historical resources in reference to the subject property is to formulate an overview of the previous uses in order to help determine whether or not the uses would lead to a Recognized Environmental Condition in connection with the subject property."

Still, doing one of these reports was like putting together a puzzle, and sometimes you had to weave in the required boilerplate legal language, technical standards, and scientific terms.

At the Wing house in those days, we were learning new ways with words. Pierrette came home from the PT clinic talking about lymphedema and vertigo. Emily once looked out the window and announced, "There's just a *theme* of ladybugs out there." One day four-year-old Julia came up to me with a fierce look on her face. She wasn't so much mad at me, I think, as interested in trying out choice bits of invective, in slinging a few riffs: *You motorcycle spit! Butter soaper! Container! You snotty ham-hack!*

But with the stuff I was learning, I could dish it right back at her: *You Polynuclear Aromatic Hydrocarbon!*

CARTOPHILIA

I'd roll off to the Library for the Metsker's Maps, and the Sanborn Maps, too, or over to Libby Photography to check out their aerial photograph collection. But we also had a trove of maps in the office, U.S. Geological Survey Topo Maps, highway maps, aquifer maps, plat maps, geological maps, and the maps and aerials in our Soil Conservation Service Survey Books. Sometimes we made our own maps, of plants in wetland areas, or of the proximity of hazardous sites to particular properties.

After a while, after reviewing map after map, I noticed something. Whenever I located a subject property on a given map of whatever sort, as I determined the various natures of the surrounding properties, these quick, barely perceptible, colors would sometimes flit through my brain.

The East seemed to be a brassy smear of sunrise with striations of strident gray.

The West was a clean and fiery red, a sunset that could hold liquids, with long skinny shadows reaching towards the viewer.

The South was more of a hazy, curvaceous orange, ticklish and careless with heat and soft yellow puddles.

The North was bracing, a wave of an almost lush grey, deepening to blue-black. There were mothwing flakes of white and a surprising touch of iron green.

DEATH

From another list in the back pages: John D. McDonald referred to Death as the Green Ripper. For Henry James, Death was the Distinguished Thing, and for William Ernest Henley, the Ruffian on the Stair. Tchaikovsky called Death the Snub-Nosed Horror. John Irving talked about the Undertoad, and then there was the Man in the Bright Nightgown, from W.C. Fields. One day while cruising the glossary of the *Environmental Engineering Dictionary* (C. Lee, Ph.D. – 2nd Edition), I came across another definition: "*Death* means the lack of reaction of a test organism to gently prodding."

Hmmm. Well, that was a view. Turned out the term in this case had something to do with brine shrimp and toxicity tests. Still . . .

BUGS

Maybe we didn't always do the best job of explaining to Clients and other interested parties what we were trying to do with our various projects. In Moses Lake, my colleague Doug was interviewed by a reporter while he was ramrodding the landfarming of a pile of petroleum-contaminated soil. The idea with landfarming is that you periodically turn over and aerate the soil, to accelerate the biodegradation of the contaminants, but during the interview, Doug must have referred to the microorganisms involved as "bugs." Anyway, the story in the newspaper explained that Doug planned to handle the situation by releasing petroleum-eating insects that would later be captured and killed.

SOILS ARE NOT DIRT!

It's hard to explain to lay people the affection that Environmental Consultants sometimes have for USDA Soil Conservation Service Survey Books. It's like telling someone why you like jazz.

There were sound technical reasons for referring to the soil books in our work, because drainage and permeability and infiltration rates and water holding capacity and the depth to the water table were good things to know when considering the potential migration of contaminants. Plus, the books sometimes had old aerial photos that made good references.

As a bonus, the Soil Conservation Service had come up with these admirably musical names for the soils. There was the Jughandle Variant and the Nicodemus Variant, the Ritzville Association and the Lawyer-Tannahill Association. I wrote reports that considered the very rocky Dragoon complex, the coarse sandy Bong-and-Phoebe, and a couple of silty loams, both Brickle and Cocalalla. I mulled over the Smackout loam, the Zen silt loam and the very cobbly Lickskillet loam. You could keep on going with the classifications, by the way. The Zaza loam was well drained and moderately permeable, and formed of weathered basalt mixed with loess. The Santa Variant was a coarse-silty, mixed, frigid Fragic Haploxeralf. Now the Shebang silt loam happened to be a fine smectitic mesic Xeric Argialboll. Question: was it or was it not montmorillonic?

A STUDY IN GREEN

As I've said, I didn't consider the work I was doing as actually engaging in some sort of profession—I tended to sleepwalk through it too much for that, the more so as the years wore on.

But I did like that sense of arcane knowledge, of being all boned up on X, keyed in on shop talk and backstage bandy-about.

Sometimes, I almost felt like the scholar I'd imagined I could have been in college, as I pored over the names of previous owners on the Maps, or in the City of Spokane Polk's Directories, as I searched for evidence of drycleaners or foundries or electroplaters on a given property. And as I scribbled seedful names into the back of my current Elan: Columbus Quesenberry . . . Jennifer Elf . . . Prince Trihub . . . Freelove Baskette . . . Antoinette Fantasia. I found ambiguous names: Euphemia McGregor . . . Tenal Fractious . . . Exilda Stonestreet. And alliterative names: Pepper P. Pendleton . . . Brandy Beanblossom. Even heroic names: Buzz Bloodgood . . . Robert Goodspeed . . . Tina Broadsword . . . Rex Rainbolt . . . Ace Earthman. (Actually, I met Ace at a party one night).

Or like a detective. A literary detective, anyway. I never shadowed anyone, and no one bonked me on the head, but I'd do leg work. I'd check sources. I'd inspect dim archives and sneezy files in the backrooms and vaults of the County Auditor's Office or the City Building Permit Department or the Fire Department.

Or I'd go to Pioneer Title, a private company that as a courtesy let guys like me look at the Tract Books. Now the Tract books were huge, what they called elephant folios, and they could have been bound in elephant hide, or some such thick and crackly old leather. Some of them were over 100 years old. Still, they were used all the time, with the searchers leaning on the counters—do I actually remember a brass rail?—as they fanned through pages the color of tea and with the aroma of cheese, checking for quit claim deeds and warranty deeds, covenants and easements and lawsuits, and boundary disputes and tax delinquency and sheer cussed chicanery. Environmental consultants had to look at these things in a green light, of course.

In a way, my visits and those of the other searchers were just last hurrahs before Internet fever changed title research forever. I do hope the Tract Books survived. They were tough books, and maybe they're in some crypt deep below Pioneer Title. The properties themselves, now, they certainly abide, though the people involved come and go, like a crop. Or maybe we could view money as the crop, and people as "no more than the compost in which dollars grow, ripen, fall, and grow again" (Tom Disch).

One day in one of the books, I came across the story of Myrtle who'd been declared insane, and her husband appointed guardian of her affairs. This husband, a certain Charles, purchased on Myrtle's behalf, presumably with Myrtle's money, Lots 1 and 2 of the Huckleberry Addition. Later, again on Myrtle's behalf, Charles sold Lots 1 and 2 to a woman named Jeanne. Then Charles went ahead and divorced Myrtle. I knew this because Lots 1 and 2 were mentioned in the divorce settlement: Myrtle, or her lawyer, fought for the Lots, but it was too late. Next thing I knew, Charles married Jeanne and all transactions involving the Lots thereafter were carried out by Charles. Appalling. I looked around the big busy room, wishing I knew someone well enough to roll my eyes with. But it was a serious place, people were working. For example, I was supposed to be looking for an old gas station.

But I later wondered if anyone had ever written an environmental murder mystery? *A Study in Green*, they could have called it. Or if they wanted to go hard-boiled, *The Long Green* (since money was involved) with a sleuth like Philip Marlowe or Sam Spade or Lew Archer.

Or maybe the sleuth could have been Jack Hazard, this Spokane P.I. I'd discovered in one of the old Polk's Directories. Or maybe Dashiell Hammett himself, who'd worked as a detective in Spokane for six or seven months in 1920, as a Pinkerton. But despite a diligent investigation, I never could find him.

JUST ANOTHER SHOT

I didn't write *A Study in Green*, but I snatched random chunks of time to write a Young Adult Novel, *The Legend of Vanilla Godzilla*. Just taking another shot at making money. When my kids themselves were young adults. More or less. I had hopes of *Vanilla Godzilla* catching on with some agent, and then with some pub-lisher, and then maybe with someone who'd take a movie flyer on the thing. And give me money. Which we could always use. But I never received the least nibble from an agent, and the manuscript is in a filing cabinet somewhere in the basement. However, I did get paid a couple hundred bucks for writing a freelance environmental article called *Vapor Intrusion/Vapor Encroachment: A Look at ASTM's New Standard Guide.*

I entered the "Describe the Perfect Pint of Guinness" contest. Maybe I could win a pub in Ireland. And then I could sell the pub, for money, and that would be good. I imagined that to win an Irish pub you had to pour on the poetry. I imagined being inside the pub, with *weather at the window, soft as gauze,* while I sat listening to *the fire's glimmering applause.* And then when someone arrived with the Pint, I'd describe *the crown of smoky snow* and *the last dark ruby drop down below,* and conclude that *by the time we find the Perfect Guinness . . . it's in us.*

I didn't win. Maybe they saw through me, and could tell I'd never liked Guinness, never.

YOU'RE THE EXPERT

Things kept happening in the industry—there were the random, everyday layoffs, and then the dot-com bubble and after that the Great Recession—and so my little green niche pretty much disappeared. You could say that the Internet got me. And/or the electronic re-engineering of Finding Things Out. Regulatory agency searches, historical research, and chain-of-title examinations now tended to be outsourced to specialized information services that sometimes delivered these gigantic data packages that with documentation could run to 400, 500 pages, when printed out, and we had to print them out. Sometimes it seemed that these services operated under the theory that whoever came up with the heaviest report would be the winner. Sometimes in defense, we touted local knowledge as a selling point, with the idea that the technoplasmic tendrils had only reached so far, so far. But the handwriting was on the wall, and I was sixty years old.

So I started writing résumés, office work résumés, environmental research résumés, résumés so diffuse and general there was a chance that whoever read them might be led to assume I could do practically anything. And I was networking and looking at want ads and bulletin boards, the kind of things you do,

Then it turned out that after my long marination in the industry—and after I raised my game with training—I just might be qualified to be an actual full-time Environmental Professional. The idea was that I'd learn to do site visits myself, rather than just making my standard ESA research moves while contemplating the ghosts of properties on maps or in books or in files. And, anyway, college—and retirement, hopefully—were on the horizon.

So I did it, became an Environmental Professional. They gave me a Certificate that said this was so. Sometimes I felt I'd received the Certificate in much the way that, instead of an actual heart, the Tin Woodman was awarded a ticking, heart-shaped Testimonial on a chain. On my first solo site visit, I asked a guy a question about some process or other, and he shrugged and said, "You're the expert."

AHERA

I took AHERA (Asbestos Hazard Emergency Response Act) training because I had to know where asbestos might possibly be in a given structure, and sometimes I'd have to take samples of suspect materials and send them to labs. I'd end up taking all sorts of other samples, of earth and air and water, for my upgraded job, but nothing made me as nervous as taking asbestos samples.

But asbestos really was and is a wonder. Legend had it—our AHERA instructor said—that Charlemagne had a tablecloth woven of asbestos. After a bacchanal, they'd just throw the tablecloth into a roaring fire to burn away the stains, all the party impurities.

They'd fish the thing out when it was clean and bright and ready to boogie again.

Beyond that, beyond being a famously spinnable, weavable and unburnable mineral, asbestos is flexible, light and stable. Asbestos can absorb and filter, is a great heat insulator, and has low electrical conductivity. Asbestos is stronger than steel and practicably indestructible—and murderously hazardous. Those marvelously fine fibers? Finer than a human hair, and capable of shredding into even finer fibers, fine enough to remain suspended 72 hours in still air? Our instructor said, *Those fibers are uncoughable.* That scary word remained with me. You can't cough up the fibers, and if you do come down with asbestosis, you can't cough up the inflammation and the scars. And you can't cough up tumors.

So I had this fear that never really left me (and maybe that was a good thing) when the time came for me to take samples myself. I wondered, Have I sampled everything that needed to be sampled? Could something dreadful be hidden deep in the bowels of a structure?

And over the years, they'd put asbestos in so many materials. One estimate said it had been used, to one degree or another, in *3,000* different products. The prize, though, probably went to Kent Cigarettes and their famous micronite filter of the 1950s. Micronite! When I was a kid, when I saw the ads on TV, I had to wonder if *micronite* was somehow related to *kryptonite*, except that upon exposure, Superman would just grow smaller and smaller and smaller, a la *The Incredible Shrinking Man.* And remember, these were *Kent* cigarettes. Were they trying to establish a connection with *Clark* Kent? (And I'd heard that smoking stunted your growth, was *that* a connection?)

But we learned in AHERA class that Kent's micronite filter had been manufactured with crocidolite blue asbestos, the worst of the worst. So when you smoked Kents, these forever fibers, those indestructible fibers that would never come out of the lungs—

uncoughable, remember?—would get coated in carcinogens on their way in. So what else is there to say about that?

A SITE VISITOR

So I started ranging out of the office for a company called Blue Mountain, all over the Northwest, all day, doing site visits, and sometimes visiting libraries for that local knowledge. After a few site visits, I got the feeling I could walk in and wander around anywhere with a hard hat, a clipboard, a camera, and maybe one of those orange or green fluorescent vests, and nobody would ask questions. Oh, and if anybody happened to be in a mood to scrutinize, I could point out my steel-toed boots. To really impress someone—impress them into a panic, maybe—I could don my handy respirator mask. Or, to get the language right, my elastomeric full facepiece respirator.

I never did end up wearing it on a job, though I'd passed my fit test. For that, I'd recited the Gettysburg Address while wearing the mask while a guy waved around a vial of banana oil (isoamyl acetate). I was supposed to tell him if I could smell it.

On a site, I'd walk around and search for telltale signs, stains, residues, corrosion, odors, distressed vegetation. I'd look for drains and pits and wells and drums and tanks. I'd collect the questionnaire I'd sent out previously, I'd do interviews. Eventually, it seemed to me I could capsulize what I needed to know simply enough: How does the hazardous stuff, if any, come onto this property, what does it do on this property, if anything, and how does it ever leave, if it ever does? Might something be left behind? Or had something been left behind long ago? And just how hazardous are we talking here?

The one thing I truly did become an expert at was running my stuff past Blue Mountain's German engineer, a kind, courtly man who gave everybody's work careful attention all week. On the weekends, he liked to race off to Portland in his Mercedes, roaring around the curves of the Columbia Gorge at 90 miles an hour.

SITES

The Guy Group once did an Environmental Site Assessment of a former casket factory in a neighborhood known as Peaceful Valley. Over the years, I worked on assessments of a prosthetics clinic and a former chicken hatchery. And at a battleground near Stites, Idaho, where the Nez Perce had skirmished with the United States Army. There was that Nike missile site that someone wanted to turn into a home. I did an abandoned drive-in theater in Wenatchee, and a ranch up in the Grand Coulee country. There were plenty of offices and dozens of cell tower sites. We assessed cranberry bogs and a grass seed research facility. I remember visiting an onion processing plant and a warehouse holding ten million pounds of potatoes. We did car washes and auto lube joints and junk yards and thrift shops. Churches and lumberyards and steam plants. Gravel pits and golf courses. I checked out a spa and a Planned Parenthood clinic.

Sometimes when I was off-duty, I'd drive past some of these properties. and feel sort of in the know. Almost . . . proprietary. Affectionate? Anyway, I knew a few things about these places. I'd been behind the scenes.

DRIVING

With Blue Mountain, I had my traveling routine down. I'd buy a giant mocha from some random roadside shop, tuck the lumbar roll Pierrette had whipped up for me into the chronically sore spot in my lower left back, crank up the AC, then head down the highway with my soundtrack. Usually, I'd tune in whatever rock and roll station I could find and just let it blast away. Once in an exceptionally isolated canyon in Idaho, all I could get on the radio was a Ladies Bible Study program, and believe me, these ladies were not dynamic. On another day in central Washington, I listened to Mexican hip hop for a couple of hours. Those guys *were* dynamic, but I could never find that station again.

I ranged farther and farther from home, and I still found names in the libraries when I was on the hunt for local knowledge, on the Maps, in the Directories. I found one favorite in Cashmere, WA, a Mrs. America Newberry. She lived on Pleasant Avenue.

For certain complicated trips, getting home by nightfall wasn't always a sure thing, and I'd have to cast around for a roadside motel. I remember pushing too hard too late at night, and biting my knuckles to keep alert, hard enough to make an impression in my skin, hard enough to convert pain energy into driving vigilance, though not hard enough to draw blood.

Once I slid off the highway into a rest area so icy the car twirled all the way across the parking lot. Once the weather was so foggy, I missed my exit on the way home. Then there was the time I climbed out of mellow, partly sunny Lewiston, Idaho, rising 2,000 feet to the rim of the Clearwater Canyon to hit U.S. Route 95, and drove straight into the heart of a Palouse blizzard.

HOW GREEN?

Someone at the Guy Group had once run an environmental program in the Air Force. One day for a training exercise, he'd issued each member of his team a Geiger counter, and told them to find a low-radioactivity source he'd hidden somewhere on the base. Then he went back to his office to do paper work and occasionally contemplate the low-radioactivity source, waiting right there on his desk. The morning wore on and no one showed up at his door, so he went looking. Finally, he found his people down at the baseball field, counters clicking away. Something hotter than anything else around was buried below the pitcher's mound, and absolutely nobody knew anything about it. He could find no records. Well, the military was notoriously messy, we all knew that.

Then there was that guy in Spokane who ran a hazardous waste disposal company. Now you can take care of hazardous wastes a number of ways: you can process and recycle, you can incinerate (at a *very* high temperature, with oxygen), you can pyrolyze (at pretty much the same temperature, without oxygen), you can make various stabs at ways of sequestering the wastes forever. You could even vitrify the wastes, turn them into glass, at least a kind of glass. This guy streamlined the whole business by simply taking away every bit of the hazardous material people were paying him to remove, and then heading back to headquarters and dumping everything down a dry well. God knows what strange transmutations were steaming and burbling down there by the time he was finally busted.

And everybody had heard stories about clients mainly interested in what they could get away with, and if you didn't deliver on the wink-wink, nudge-nudge, they'd let you know they were shopping around. And maybe they'd choose the guy who was suspected of doing the occasional drive-by Assessment: "Hey, it looked good from the car window."

Of course, there's potential for abuse in everything, but the people I knew in the industry were straight shooters. Sometimes, though, I wondered about some of the straight shooting we did. How green was it for me to drive over 300 miles to a Conoco bulk plant in Helena, Montana to hand an air sample pump to a guy who'd masked up so he could place the pump in the center of a giant empty tank? Two hours later, the guy handed the pump back to me, whereupon I drove to Fed Ex so I could send the sample cartridges to a lab, before heading back to Spokane.

Did it help to save the world by bringing bad news to someone who'd already figured out his wafer-thin margin for buying a pizza parlor in Wenatchee before his bank told him to hire somebody who just might bring him bad news? (So many times, it was a bank pushing these things.) What if someone like me found an obscure mention of an underground tank on the pizza property in a City Public Works file, as I did? Then we had to hire a Ground-Penetrating Radar specialist to check for the possible tank (the guy told us he was fresh from searching for the grave of a murder victim in a field in North Dakota). Then we planned a drilling and sampling program. How wafery can a wafer-thin margin get?

At about the same time, Dupont was getting away with contaminating the drinking water of millions with PFAs.

Sometimes, I batted these questions back and forth with colleagues. Sometimes, we wondered about the whole regulation-fueled, lawyer-driven process we found ourselves caught up. Were we making a net positive difference, or were we spitting into the wind? Were the locations we were looking at simply too, well, *local?* Were we all too caught up in particular places while all around in the greater world, sly poisons were infiltrating subtle pathways? The Guy had once said that when he first studied Environmental Engineering, one of his teachers proclaimed, *Dilution is the solution to pollution.* But what if dilution was failing us? What if dilution had nowhere to go after a while, and started backing up into saturation instead? What if we were spitting into a hurricane?

We were doing stuff that needed to be done, but nobody was talking about carbon dioxide.

THE LIGHTS IN THE WINDOWS

Before I could officially retire, one last urgent project slid in under the wire, and so I found myself driving from Spokane to Moses Lake to pick up a water sampling kit, and then heading off to Quincy and beyond to take twelve water samples and to do three Environmental Site Assessments at five apple and cherry orchards, and then cruising down to Othello to drop off eight water samples at a lab there, and then returning to Moses Lake to Fed-Ex the four final water samples to another lab in Redmond, and then barreling back to Spokane, after rolling up over 400 miles. Yes, it was a very long day.

But I remember driving down the highway thinking I was almost done, with that day, with my green job. At my home office,

I'd put together my report, finishing it off with one of the standard boilerplate conclusions: *Property inspection, interviews, historical review, and review of the Environmental Database, revealed no potential environmental risks, recognized environmental conditions, or other environmental hazards.* Or, if I decided there really was something to flag, *This site may be characterized as a moderate to serious risk of an existing release, a past release, or a material threat of a release of hazardous materials to the environment.*

Or maybe I'd just write what I'd always wanted to write for a last hurrah, *Seems to me this site is hazardous enough to knock a buzzard off a gut wagon.*

At home, I'd shred my remaining business cards into confetti, but until then I was driving, driving, driving, with the sun already down.

But I can practically see the lights in the windows, Kitty Spangle and Danny Bonebright, Zelma Shining and Hall Moonbeam. *We're almost there*, Glinda Freelinger. *Just about*, Jim Sincere and Harry Tranquil and June Sleep . . .

UNDO THE FOLDS

Rain's syncopated beat
drums the tin roof.
Wind pulls back the folds of night
and a voice runs through my head.
It's better to be welcoming,
let it land like a bird
that sees it won't be caught.
A towhee swoops down for a treasure,
a tiny sarcophagus,
dried wasp in its shell of skin.
I hear the words again.
Lambs come into the world
most often at night,
slip through from another darkness
in their gooey coat,
stand within seconds
to be lick-bathed.
In the early morning
opening the barn door,
I saw the small hind legs hanging out,
reached to tie on
a piece of baling twine,
seconds fumbling
to make this mercy work,
pull it into the world,
hear the chant again.

LISTEN FOR THE BEAT

We all begin tied
to another, two heartbeats
braiding for months,
the quick one blooming
in the hollows of the slower pulse.
Three seasons and the tremor comes
when each prepares for the passage
through the gate of ischial spines,
the parting that begins
the search for a semblance
of the first union.
Grown, we comb the days
for a match, eyes that dart away
on the subway, dance-halls,
count as one of the lucky
if the old syncopation
laces the air.
Some wander like Magellan,
some go out for milk
and are gone for eleven years.
Some cannot be apart
for more than a day,
ache for the four
in the two-four beat.
For others the lacing unravels
in the alchemy of time.
But the first scar

aches to be soothed
walking the snow flattened grass,
standing alone in the kitchen.
Some hear voices, some anesthetize,
some paste a cobbled vision
on the inevitable oblivion
but in the end all the water
goes back to the sea.

AS FROG IS MY WITNESS

THIS is how the summer begins. Mama and I sit in the parlor. A cigarette hangs from her lips, smudged carmine like the clay smeared beneath my toenails from playing in the pond. Usually, Mama would be mad at me tracking dirt on her carpets, but she's in a mood, which she says is a grownup way of having a tantrum. I have tantrums sometimes, and she takes care of me, so when she's feeling bad, I take care of her, too.

Mama has a glass of wine, and a few drops smatter the collar of her blouse like fat red tears. Last summer, she let me try some, and the bitter sits heavy on my tongue every time I take a whiff. I asked her why she drank it so much, but she just puffed out smoke and smiled. I'd understand when I was older, she said. But I am older now, a whole summer older, and I still don't get it. It's just grapes.

We just sit here, all quiet, watching a log crumble in the fireplace. It's too hot, especially with the fire, but Mama likes watching the flames so she has all the windows in the house thrown open. The house gasps in the hot air, a fish out of water. Mosquitoes and cicadas have their screaming matches—Mama says they're like an orchestra, but I've never seen an orchestra. Anyways, there's not much pretty about bugs yelling at each other. A couple of the screens are out of the windows, so a few flit in, and I keep slapping at my arms to keep from getting bit. A couple times I catch a mosquito, and a big pat of blood squashes out of the body. Yuck.

"Michael," Mama finally says. She stubs out a cigarette into her little porcelain ashtray, the one painted with monarch butterflies.

"Your cousins are coming to stay for the summer."

"Oh," I say.

"Your Uncle Robert is dropping them off Tuesday."

"Oh."

Mama reaches for another cigarette, but the pack crushes empty in her hand. She tosses it into the flames with a little sigh, and the whole thing sparks and sputters into flakes of ash.

"You don't have to share a room. I'll have the maids do up the guest bedroom."

"Okay."

Mama sends away the maids in the evenings, so except for the bugs, everything is still. I like it best this way. It's a good kind of quiet. There's a different kind when Daddy's home, sort of like right between a fork of lightning and a big boom that rattles the china cabinet.

But none of that after Tuesday. There will be the girls in their flouncy dresses, all blown and inflated like dandelion puffs, and the other boys with stones stuffed in their pockets to throw at each other when no one's looking. I've got five cousins on Uncle Robert's side. They're all hard and sharp, like knives, except worse because they've got teeth. Mama says they're good kids, except because there's five of them, they've got to act up to get anyone to look at them.

"Come here, baby," Mama says.

I'm not a baby at all—in fact, I'll be twelve next spring. But I sort of don't mind when Mama lets me curl up at her feet like she does now, head in her lap so she can comb through my hair. Her wool skirt will leave little indents on my cheek, but I could fall asleep here anyways.

"Aren't you hot, Mama?" I ask.

Her fingertips drift to a stop on my scalp. "What?"

"Your skirt. That's for winter."

She laughs and ruffles my hair, and a few pieces flop across my forehead and into my eyes. "It doesn't matter all that much. This is my favorite skirt. Why shouldn't I wear it?"

I don't have much to say to that. I wear my favorite plaid shirt every day, especially when Daddy isn't home to make me wash it. Mama says as long as I don't smell like a hog in a sty, she doesn't see much use in washing something I'll just get dirty again.

Mama starts singing. She's got a pretty voice—she says she could have been famous if she hadn't gotten married and had me, and of course that's not my fault, it's her no good sonuva-you-know-what husband, and then she gets all quiet.

So sometimes Mama sings for me when Daddy's not home, which is a lot of the time. She sings in Italian, but sometimes she'll sing in French or German. She calls it opera. Tonight, she tells me her song is about a lost love, which is what all of them are. Her throat bobs with each vowel, dipping like a buoy borne by a storm. I don't really get music, but I like her songs. They're about sad things, but they don't sound sad when she sings them. I don't hear the cicadas anymore, and then I don't hear anything anymore, because before the song is over, I'm up in my bed and Mama's tucking me in tight.

SUMMER is my favorite, because I can wake up before the maids arrive and sneak off to the pond. I like to spend the whole day there, sometimes sneaking into the kitchen to snatch an apple off the counter for lunch. The pond water is muddy and murky and matted with clumps of algae that slime between my toes when I kick off my boots to go frog-catching. There are thick stands of reeds and cat-'o-nine-tails and big grasses that whip my ankles when I try to walk through. I can slide down this little bank into the water, and when I crouch down to look at the tadpoles no one can see me.

If Eden were real, it would be just like this. But I don't believe in all that. Mama says it's a bunch of phooey, because when she was little the reverends were real mean to her and told her that because she gets sad all the time it meant she had the Devil in her and didn't love God enough. But she told me to take that nonsense with a grain of salt. So I do.

This morning, I slipped my plaid shirt over my head and trekked to the pond. I've got lots to keep track of. The dragonflies are back this summer in twos, which means I might have baby dragonflies to look after soon. My favorite spends the morning sunning itself on a rock, bright green body flashing like a penny. I think about going inside to get pencil and paper to sketch it, but I don't, because today is the most important day of my life.

Today, there's a bullfrog at the pond.

There haven't been many frogs for the last few summers because they all got sick and died—croaked. Ha.

But I missed my frogs. I liked to catch them, and they'd wriggle around all warm and slimy in my hands until they calmed down, and then they didn't mind me holding them. Once, a little one peed on me, and I dropped it into the pond with a big plop and shrieked so loud Mama came running thinking I'd slipped and busted my head open. After that, though, I just knew to hold them really carefully and set them down if they started getting too squirmy, because that meant they were scared and were going to you-know-what.

But today, there's a bullfrog. He's big and round and flat and he's plopped himself in the shallow part of the pond, almost like he's sitting right on the surface. Every time he ribbets, ripples whoosh out around him, making the water-striders scramble to keep from tipping over. Every few minutes, I take another tiny step closer. He's only a little bit away now, and I'm holding my breath so he doesn't hear me coming up behind him.

Up over the hill, a car honks its horn. The bullfrog hops below the surface and I sort of droop down. I'll catch him another day, I guess.

I clamber up the side of the pond, careful not to slip in the mud. Uncle Robert's car sits pretty and sparkly in the driveway. He opens the door, and my cousins spill out in one big heap of their

Sunday best. Mama's in her nice clothes, too, and she steps off the front porch in her swishy house dress and flouncy apron with a platterful of lemonade. She laughs real high at something Uncle Robert says, which is what she does when someone says something not-funny but she feels bad.

I slide back into the pond so no one can see me. All my cousins are shouting and running around and causing a ruckus already. Mama said maybe I'll like them, and I said I didn't like them when they came for Christmas last year, and she said that I wasn't being a very gracious host. So then I went to bed.

MAMA rings the big old bell out on the porch to call me in for dinner, except it's not for dinner but to tell me to get my butt in the house and scrub all my mud off because we've got company. Otherwise she'd just walk a little down the hill and holler for me. Daddy doesn't like when she does that, says it's unladylike, but Mama doesn't mind him much. So I wonder if he's home, or if she's just being proper to set a good example for the other kids.

I sneak in through the kitchen and dart up to my room. One of the cooks giggles at me, says I'm streaking through the house like a muddy cat. I sort of giggle at that.

I strip out of my old shirt and muddy shorts and stick my head in the sink to get the pond stink out of my hair. There's mud all over my legs, so I scrub at them with an old washcloth until my skin glows strawberry. My hair drips all over my new clean clothes, the nice ones I've got for fancy dinners and church picnics. They'll get wrinkly, but my towel is all muddy so I can't do much to dry off except shake my head around like a big shaggy dog.

The stairs creak under my feet. I was expecting there to be a racket in the dining room, but instead, everything is quiet so Mama hears me coming downstairs.

"That you, Michael?"

The dining room doors are propped open with the heavy decorative urns from the hall, letting strands of sunlight in to doze on the tabletop. A wiry gray head scowls at me from the head of the table.

Mama's chin lifts, and a tiny smile struggles onto her face. "Come say hello to your Grandpa."

There's no carpet in the dining room, so my feet go *whack, whack, whack* on the cold wood floors. Five pairs of eyes and five bitter scowls follow me through the room. My hair feels very wet. A tiny drip clings to my eyebrow then lets go. It slides down my nose, hangs for a second, then splats onto my bare feet.

"Hello, Grandpa," I say, real fast and low so I can get it over with.

Mama thwacks me on the back of my head. "Mind your manners."

I got in trouble last year for mumbling in class. Lots of grown ups don't like how I talk to them, because I'm too quiet or don't look at them or talk so fast my words snarl up into one big knot. So Mama taught me to say all my words like holding a frog: careful and slow, so you don't spook them and make them pee.

"Hello, Grandpa. How are you?" I try again.

"I'm well, thank you. Now, sit so we can all say grace and eat. You've kept us waiting long enough," Grandpa says.

I squeak out the empty chair next to Grandpa, which I don't mind so much because Mama's opposite of me. Grandpa drops his hands face up on the table. They're warm and wet like meat left out too long. I ease my hand into his, and Colette takes my other hand. Mama says grace, slow like she's very extremely grateful, but I know it's because we don't say grace much when Daddy's not home and she has to think hard about what to say.

"Amen," says Grandpa, and Colette, too. I mouth it.

There's lots of rules to remember about fancy dinners, so I don't listen much to the conversation. But it's not much of a conversation, anyway, because it's just Grandpa talking and then Mama going *mhm.*

There's green beans in front of me, so I scoop out just a little bit without bumping Colette with my elbow then pass it on. Then mashed potatoes, and I don't scrape the serving spoon off with my fork but scoop and plop instead, except I have to make sure not to shower everyone with potato flakes when I do the plop. And then there's the ham on a big platter, and Grandpa serves that, so I pass my plate up and don't say anything bad about how much he gave me, even though I think ham is stinky and Mama wouldn't make me eat it if it were just us two. But I'll eat everything on my plate, because of the starving children and the economy and all that.

I concentrate and pour salt all over my plate and wolf it all down. Colette looks at me funny, so I look at her funny back. She looks silly, anyhow. She's got on a pink dress with all sorts of ribbons and a thick, fluffy petticoat even in the heat. Mama never gets that dolled up, not even for church.

Mama's foot nails me in the shin out of nowhere. My head shoots up fast. "Yes?"

"You listen when I'm talking to you, boy," Grandpa says.

"Yes, sir."

"You respect your elders."

"Yes, sir."

"Don't you want to be saved?"

"Yes sir."

Mama hisses through her teeth. Wrong answer. Except I do want to be saved from lots of things, namely drowning and housefires and this awful, tricky dinner full of traps.

"George and I haven't discussed it yet," Mama says. "We want to make sure he's ready."

Grandpa fixes his meanest stare on her. "My son is a good, Christian man. He wants his son to be baptized so he can be with his Lord. Do you want my grandchild going to the devil?"

Colette fidgets beside me. "You ain't been baptized yet?"

"No, I *haven't*," I say. Mama says you ain't supposed to say ain't.

"You're a sinner." Colette's eyes go wide. "Dirty," she whispers.

"And you look like a stuffed pig, but you don't hear anyone making a fuss about it."

Big, wet tears well up like magic in her eyes. Her cheeks get red as if she'd been slapped, and she throws her blonde head into her hands. Across the table, Donald stops picking on his baby brother and gives me a nasty look, but Grandpa is too busy yelling at Mama to notice.

Grandpa's voice gets loud and scary. "George didn't raise his boy for you to encourage wickedness in his soul."

"George didn't raise squat," Mama shouts back.

And Grandpa lifts his big slab of a hand, and it whooshes through the dining room, and Mama doesn't even have time to flinch before she gets hit.

There's a big, burning handprint on Mama's cheek. Grandpa doesn't say a word. Even Colette's gone silent. I reach my hand to her, but Mama stands up quick, rattling the silverware on the table.

"Time for bed. Say goodbye to your Grandpa," Mama says, and then she takes her plate into the kitchen and doesn't come back. MAMA'S door is still open when I go upstairs. I creep inside, curtains rustling softly like old, dry leaves on the carpet. My feet swish when I walk, but Mama pretends like she doesn't hear me.

Grandpa's voice is loud and low from in the parlor. He and the other big kids stayed downstairs while he drank from Daddy's locked cabinet in the kitchen, and so it's too loud to sleep.

I creep into bed beside Mama and pull the sheets up to my chin. Sometimes, this side of the bed smells like Daddy—sharp aftershave and old sweat—but he's been gone too long for there to be anything other than a tiny whiff of pine.

"Go to bed, baby," Mama whispers.

"I'm not tired."

Mama doesn't move, so I lift myself on my elbows and peer at her face. Her mascara is smeared and her lipstick is wisped to the corner of her mouth from when she got hit. Her eyes are open, but she's not really looking at anything.

"Mama?"

Crickets chirp outside. The windows are still open from the other day, but it's not so hot anymore so I'm glad I crawled under the covers. The sound downstairs is dying down—Grandpa gets tired when he drinks—so the other kids will be coming to bed soon.

"Mama," I say, and when she keeps quiet, "I guess I'm going to bed."

I slip out of the covers and pad out the door. I half expect to hear Mama call me back, or tell me goodnight, but she doesn't make a peep. The door eases shut behind me.

The old muddy towel and dirty clothes are still on my bedroom floor. I pile them all up into a basket so the maids don't fuss when they come to clean my room. Then I decide to straighten up my sheets from the tangle I made last night, then I line my shoes up in a neat little line by the wall, then I shut the window and do the latch up the way Mama used to do when I would open them and lean out so far I almost fell out.

Grandpa walks down the driveway. His knee buckles and folds like a rusted hinge. He served, Daddy says. Ambulance driver. He got the truck shot out from under him twice, and the second time the gear stick stabbed up his knee so bad he got sent home for good.

Grandpa has a bundle of white under his arm. The cloth loosens and flaps to the ground, sputtering over the gravel drive, a stiff little triangle dragging the dirt. They almost look like sheets.

Smoke sizzles on the breeze, but I can't see what's burning. I shut the window.

MAMA didn't come out of her room this morning. But I can hear her from the pond. That's because the pond is behind the house, and so is Mama's room, and her windows are still open so I can hear her singing. I guess she doesn't want to be bothered.

This morning, she's singing in French. Everybody thinks French is pretty, but it's all hacky and rough, sort of muttery like how I talk. Everybody gives me grief about not speaking up, so how come it's nice when you're French? I asked Mama once, and she laughed and said *c'est la vie*. That's life.

The bullfrog is back this morning. Except I'm not trying to catch it. Instead, I roll my pants up past my knees and wade out through the muck to the middle of the pond. It's not that deep—not deep enough for fish, anyhow—but it's deep enough that Mama doesn't like me walking through the middle, where the mud grabs at my ankles and doesn't want to let go. But she's not paying me any mind, and I'm bigger now, anyhow, so I go through the middle.

"What are you doing?"

I have to tug at my knees to get myself turned around. Colette and Donald and the little ones are splayed out in a ring, all fuzzy looking because they're standing way back clear of the cat-o'-nine-tails. They're all up high, ringed with sunlight so shadows fall murky on their confused-looking faces.

"You deaf?" Donald says.

"No," I say.

Colette stamps her pink-slippered foot. "I said, what are you doing?"

"Watching my frog."

She wrinkles up her nose. "It's ugly."

I turn around, lifting up my knees again. The mud lets go of my feet with two loud smacks. The frog is just sitting there, getting warm and happy on his rock. He's brown and bumpy. I didn't know that made something ugly.

A stone sails over my head and smacks off the shore. The bull-frog croaks in protest, but he doesn't budge.

Donald swears. "I almost got it."

"Get it!" Colette shrieks. "I don't want it near me. Get it, get it!"

"Don't hurt him," I say.

"Why not?" Donald tosses a stone between his hands. "You like it?"

"It's my friend."

The little kids snicker and laugh real loud, hollering so loud I wonder why Mama doesn't yell out for them to leave me be. But she doesn't.

"You can't be friends with a frog."

"Daddy says animals aren't God's creatures. You're consorting with the devil," Colette snips. She crosses her arms over the ruffles on her chest. "And you ain't even baptized."

"So?"

Donald throws another rock. This one smacks off my brow, sharp and pointy, and I almost cry, but Mama says you've got to look tough so people don't give you grief, so I don't.

"Grandpa says you're a heathen," he says, and he throws another rock. He lobs a big, nasty rock. It flies up, up, up, and then all the sudden there's no more ribbets. Just a few toes wiggling sort of weakly. And then no wiggles at all.

Then they walk away.

THE air in the house is hot and heavy. The maids have got all the windows shut, and Mama screamed and screamed at them, then pretty Isobel told her Grandpa had told them to do so because Mr. Smith is coming home, then Mama smacked her across the mouth. She told her to mind her place, except then she went upstairs and locked herself in her room without opening any windows.

The cook caught me sneaking through the kitchen and told me to wash my face. I did. But my eye is all puffy and swollen, and I couldn't quite get the gunky blood out of my eyebrow. I look nice and clean if it weren't for that.

I sneak around the house playing a game I call Cat and Mouse. I'm the Mouse. I'm real quick and small and sneaky, so no one sees me when I nick slices of cheese from the refrigerator or tip-toe past the guest bedroom to spy on Colette doing her devotions. Everybody else is the Cat, except for Mama, and they don't even know it. That way I get to play my games with people and they can't say no, because they play it all the time without me having to ask.

I kinda wish Mama was playing. I wouldn't mind so much if she found me.

All the maids are whispering, *Mr. Smith, Mr. Smith*. There's always a kerfuffle when he comes home, because no one can remember if he likes sugar in his iced tea or his pillows fluffed once or twice. Pretty Isobel's still all teary from when Mama hit her. I feel bad, but I can't apologize or anything, because then I'd lose Cat and Mouse.

I can hear the gravel drive crunching even with the windows shut. Then the engine goes *clunk* and then nothing, then a few seconds later the front door creaks open. Keys clank into the bowl by the door. Shoes, *thump thump* as he kicks them off.

All these little feet go running down stairs, nobody noticing me. I'm in my least favorite spot, between Daddy's stiff leather armchair and the glass parlor door flung open into the room. I don't like it much because you can see me when you go into the parlor, but it means I can see everything going on in the hall and the dining room.

Daddy says hello to all my cousins. Donald shakes his hand all gentlemanlike, and Colette does a little curtsy and blushes when Daddy says she looks like a peony in her pretty pink dress.

Donald and Colette take the little ones away after baby Denny starts fussing for nap time. And I want to creep away, because since I'm playing Mouse I can't stay too long or I'll get caught, except instead of going upstairs Daddy comes into the parlor.

"Come out of there, Michael."

The game is up. My face goes hot and red and I crawl out from behind the chair.

"Let me see you. Stand up straight," Daddy says.

I do. I stretch my spine like there's a ruler jammed in the back of my pants. I've got all sorts of questions, like how was New York, and how long are you staying, and did you miss me, and how long until you leave again, but Daddy doesn't like when I talk too much. He says children should be seen and not heard, but if he wanted kids to look at how come he's gone so much? I don't ask that either.

Daddy sits, and his chair creaks under him like an old man popping his knees after staying still for a long time. I don't sit, because I'm not supposed to unless Daddy says so.

But he doesn't let me sit. Instead, he says, "What did you do to your face?"

I touch the cut under my eyebrow. It's wet and squishy like a squashed caterpillar. "I fell," I say.

I'm lying, of course. Mama would be able to tell, because I squeeze my hands to touch the middle of my palms to make sure they're not all sweaty, which is what happens when people lie. Except he doesn't know that, so he believes me.

"Go tell your mother that I'm home. I'd like dinner at five."

I nod and dart out of there. The stairs protest beneath me, and I think about them splitting and opening up into this big, gaping hole that swallows me up. But they don't. Instead, I get to the top and Donald laughs when I race by.

"Run, little froggy," he yells.

I show him the finger that Mama shows Grandpa when he's not looking.

Mama's door shut at the end of the hall. Quiet. She's not singing, but she's not walking around or dancing, either. She does that sometimes. Mama used to be a ballerina. I knock on the door, and nobody says anything.

"Daddy's home," I say.

Nothing. "He says he wants dinner at five."

Then, real quiet, "Go away."

So I do.

DADDY wakes me up this morning. We're going to church. It takes a while to find a pair of un-rumpled pants and a nice shirt without pond goo all over it. Daddy's car putzes in the drive, gurgling on smoke and oil that sometimes drips onto the gravel in thick rivers of tar.

Grandpa's already at church. He's the reverend. He's got to get ready, putting on his stiff black robes and rereading all the lines about Hell. That's all he ever talks about. Do this and that and you'll writhe around like worms on hot pavement for all of eternity, the end. You gotta get baptized, then you're good. But Mama didn't want me getting baptized. She's used up lots of excuses: Michael doesn't know how to hold his breath, Michael can't swim, Michael's got this scalp condition and can't get his head wet. And Daddy wasn't around to make me. So it never happened.

I tip-toe downstairs and into the kitchen. Daddy says you can't have breakfast before church, because you've got to take communion first thing. Or else you're tainted. But Colette said I'm already tainted because of the whole no baptism thing, and I'm hungry, so who cares.

The kitchen is almost empty. All the maids have Sunday morning off and don't come back until it's time to make dinner. So there's no cook, no pretty Isobel cleaning the dishes, but Mama's here.

She's got out a knife but no cutting board. Her face looks cold and wet, like leftover ham, but ham's mostly pink and Mama's face is all white.

"Mama?" I say.

"Go to church," she says, not looking up.

"I missed you."

"Go."

Daddy shouts from the front door. "Hurry up, boy."

Mama doesn't move. I guess she isn't going. I think about that knife. Knife and no cutting board. I'm not sure what that means.

"Coming," I say, and I race out the door and slam it behind me.

I DON'T go to the middle of the pond anymore. Mama was right. But it's easier to hear her singing from the edge, anyways, like she is today. Italian, I think, because every other word sounds like something yummy. *O mio carbonara, il mio bambino mozzarella, ami la mia gorgonzola.*

The back of my pants clings wet to my skin, cold and muddy. I left my shoes up in the grass so I could stretch my feet into the pond and nudge pebbles with my toe. Teeny tiny tadpoles swim around my ankles, wriggling in the murk and playing with their brothers and sisters. Gnats whisper all sorts of things in my ear. The air is just as hot as my arms and legs, and the longer I sit, it feels like I'm melting and floating up all at once, more like I'm a ghost at the pond than a person. It's nice.

The gnats keep talking to me. They're nasty. "You sleazy good-for-nothing," a girl gnat hums.

"Why do you think I leave?" a boy gnat buzzes. "At least I come back, you ungrateful buzz."

"You have a son. Did you ever think about that?"

"He's not the only one."

"Buzz you. I'll kill you."

"You're crazy. You'd get locked up if it wasn't for me."

"You think I'm crazy?"

"You're psychotic. I don't even know you anymore. You're not the woman I married, you're… you're some animal."

"I'm what you made me."

"You've been a psycho buzz since I met you."

"Buzz off, motherbuzzer."

I shoo the gnats away. They keep talking. I wish Mama would shut her window.

I DON'T come when the dinner bell rings. I'm not hungry, because I packed a sandwich and an apple. I threw the core in the pond, but there aren't any fish to eat it, so it'll just get nibbled at by bugs, and then get mushy and gross, and then it'll just be seeds, and maybe in a hundred years there'll be a big apple tree in the middle of the pond.

"Michael? Michael?" Colette yells. I hear her searching through the field, her big dress swooshing in the grass and probably startling all sorts of critters.

"Come out, little froggy," Donald says.

It's like playing Cat and Mouse, except the mean old Cats already know where I like to hide. I think about army-crawling up out of the pond and through the yard, but they'd see me. Instead, I squeeze my eyes tight and cross my fingers that they'll go away.

"Hello, little froggy."

Footsteps slide down to the pond. Rocks skitter against my legs, and I try my hardest not to flinch. I feel Donald looking at me, breathing hot at the top of my head. I keep my eyes shut.

"Don't touch him," Colette whines. "He's filthy."

"Naw, he's not that bad," Donald says, real quietly. "He just needs cleaned off a little."

Donald grabs the back of my shirt in a big, sweaty fist. Colette starts screaming, high and excited, and I picture her shrinking up into a yippy little Chihuahua foaming at the mouth in a big pile of petticoats.

I slap at Donald's hand, but he only holds on tighter. I scramble up onto my knees, and then he pitches me forward until I'm hanging from my shirt collar. The fabric yanks at my skin. I gulp real big. My nose quivers just above the pond, fuzzy algae tickling my nostrils.

"Dunk him, Donald!" Colette says, high and breathless.

"We're doing you a favor," Donald says. "You ain't been baptized, have you?"

I don't say anything. Don't even open my eyes. Maybe if I seize up, I'll get stiff and stony and so heavy he drops me and runs away, because that would be scary. Then I'd melt back into skin and stuff and brush myself off and get back to sitting at my pond.

"Well? I knew you were dumb, but I know you ain't deaf."

My throat's gone dry. I try to swallow, but my throat bobs painfully against the collar of my shirt. "Mama says you ain't supposed to say ain't."

Donald drops my shirt. Water gushes up my nose and into my ears, bitter with gunk and silt. Rocks bite into my cheek, and mud flushes up in between my teeth. When I was little, I didn't have any reflexes around the water, so I'd just breathe it all in if my mouth dipped underneath. I can hold my breath now.

So I do. I do and I do and I do.

My hands slide in the muck, and I try to press myself up, but Donald's got a hand smashed into the back of my head and everytime I try to push away my hands slip out, and my feet flail around on the shore without ever finding a grip, and I can hear Colette's exhilarated screams even through the warbled bubble of the water, and all the sudden I can't hold my breath anymore and my lungs suck up pondscum like a vacuum.

Donald hauls me up. He says something, but I don't hear, so he gets fed up and drops me in the dirt. He scrambles up the bank, laughing, and Colette's piercing laugh fades to a dull little whistle.

I open my eyes. Little drops of water cling to my eyelashes and make the world all fuzzy. Clouds wobble across the blue, staggering on big gusts of wind that smooth the grit from my face. A dragonfly—or maybe a moth—flits by. The grasses are just a green smear fogged around my vision. It's nice. Pretty.

Something hops by my feet. It's big and flat like a river stone. Then it ribbits. I knew my bullfrog didn't get squashed. He's too smart for that. He's like me. *You and me, we bounce back,* Mama used to say when she talked to me. I wonder if she'd say that now, but then I think that she wouldn't because she doesn't care as much as she used to. Not sure why.

There's dirt and grime caked onto my shirt, my knees, my face, and I'm not sure what Donald and Colette mean because I don't feel clean. I just feel sad. Then the sun drifts down, and I feel cold.

I DON'T fall asleep right there in the mud, even though I want to. Instead, I crawl out of the pond and walk barefoot to the house, shiny like a big goose egg on the hill. The door is unlocked. I'm glad about that, because sometimes Daddy puts the deadbolt on. I'm careful on the stairs, then extra quiet when I go past Donald and Colette's room, but they're sleepy and snoring so they wouldn't have heard me anyway.

My bedroom door whooshes open easy. There's a snoozing mound on my bed, snoring soft. Little curls of hair peep out from under the blankets. I try to kick off my boots without making a sound, but they clunk on the floor and the shadow on my bed stirs.

"Michael? Is that you, baby?"

I creep close to the bed. Mama's face is dark and cloudy, burrowed deep under my quilts. Her eyes are swollen and red like she's been crying.

"Mama."

She lifts the blankets. There's a spot beside her, and it looks all nice and warm. "Come here. Let me hold you."

But I don't want to.

"I'm going to go sleep in the parlor," I say. So I do.

DADDY loads us kids up in a car. He and Grandpa let me sit up in the front with them, and I don't slide around on the seat so much because I'm squeezed tight between them. Daddy smells nice, sharp—he must've shaved this morning. Grandpa smells like dirt, but that's because he's old and all old people smell like dirt. But I keep that to myself.

The car bumps through the woods, leaping over sticks and rocks to the river. *'Bout time,* Grandpa said before we left. I figure it is, too.

The engine goes *one, two, put!* then goes quiet. "Everybody out," Daddy says.

I'm dressed in my Sunday best. I'm real careful not to smudge mud on my nice shoes. Isobel bleached out all the stains on my shirt, so I don't smell like nasty pond water either. Daddy asked her to, and she giggled and said yes. Daddy likes her, and she likes him, and it's grown up stuff so it's none of my business.

Grandpa has me kick off my shoes, then my socks, then we squelch down into the deepest part of the river. The mud suctions at my toes. Donald and Colette keep the little kids quiet and still, and Daddy watches with a big hand on Mama's shoulder because she hasn't been allowed to leave her room because he says she might run away, so she's real skinny and I think maybe he's worried she might float off. But she doesn't.

Grandpa grabs my shoulders. "Do you take Jesus Christ to be your Lord and savior?"

I nod my head. "I do."

"And do you wish to repent for your sins so that you may enter into the Kingdom of Heaven?"

"I do."

He grins real proud. "By the power vested in me, I hereby baptize you in the name of the Father, the Son, and the Holy Spirit."

I go down, down, down. Water chugs through my lips, even though I keep them tight. Grandpa's got his hands sandwiched on my chest, one keeping me from sinking and the other keeping me from getting out of the water. I've got to get good and clean. But it's dark, and I keep thinking about the cold, wet feeling in my lungs just creeping up until I'm holding my breath so tight my head feels like it might pop off and float away.

And then I come up. Everybody's singing an old baptism song in English. That's the only language I know, and it's the language of our Lord and Nation, so it's the best one. Well, everybody's singing except for Mama, because the doctors say she needs to rest for her nerves and not do anything that will excite her, so she's supposed to keep quiet.

Grandpa pats me on the back, and that's that. *It's about time*, I think as I climb out of the river. It's August now, and I've got to go back to school, and I can't do that if I'm dirty. But now I'm living properly. No more mucking around in the pond, no more opera, no more acting like a kid. I'm a man in the eyes of the Lord, now.

And that's how the summer ends.

origin of hate

slavery is a bad idea. (jericho brown)

it brought night to the room of history,
it pushes us into the questions of wrong or right,
yesterday i had to uproot every lily in my garden
they remind me of cannons, short guns, mirrors and vases
and how they are worth more than my fathers.

slavery is a very bad idea, it is the origin of all hatred,
it ruined the person of sea, and made moth into the poetry of grief,
every father that died turned dove, soiling the doves' reputation;
birds hovering with odes to the home they cannot be,
ask me what it did to me. it cast dark spells unto every line of my
poetry;

i should be writing a poem for my unborn daughter; faatimah
but here i am, retelling the tales of my great-grandmother; faatimah
caught on her way to the stream by lord henry and the slavers,
i do not know what to tell this daughter about her great-grandmother;
who was moon, only one night left never to come back

VICTORY

O how I want to loose thunder
on the scrotal sac of females throbbing

birthsongs in the eave of my porch.
Below their paper palace, I long to

press the Hot Shot button, spray
brimstone until my arm goes numb,

until the harrowing hum, the death
in their asses, drops silent, one by one.

My trigger finger twitches, remembers
spit and tobacco daubed on stings,

the bitter cure equal to the agony.
I want to kill them all—but hold my fire

for the sake of their exquisite architecture,
their warrior hearts and aim, slings

and arrows for the just and wanton alike,
angels of squash bloom and zinnia.

I hold for the sake of our waning, burning
world, for clearing karma of past lives

to the next, for mothers huddled in blind
ecstasy, daughters breech in their sweet

hexagons, my windows and bare feet
so near the sleek poison, nearer still

our mutual deliverance.

UNSHUTTERED

I push aside the lace, so photogenic in the village,
often with cats sunning in the sill, turn the knob

hard left to unclasp the seven-foot windows
of this 19th century country farm. I've learned

to work the inner shutter's intricate contraption
and finally fling it open to cool morning,

low talk of pilgrims on *le chemin* through
to Spain, tap-tapping their walking sticks.

The ancient speaks loudest: the crumbling wellhouse,
earthenware cast from the Garonne's clay banks,

the clock tower striking slow hours. All set
against the lot of RVs traveling Europe

on a whim, Brits complaining of visas for only
ninety days—while I, comfortable in my room

or sleek studio, cast unhurried lines to sink
or swim where the current runs calm, listen

for tawny owls at nightfall, the bass notes
of doves to unclasp whatever burdens still

weigh or speak in languages though foreign
to my ear, uncomplicate my stony path.

THE MISSING LINK

WHEN the doorbell rang, I was in my room pretending to put on a holiday sweater while actually playing my fifth consecutive hour of Super Mario Brothers. In those days I had a Nintendo with an 8-bit processor, a now-stone-age machine that generated about fourteen colors and shoddy audio, as if every sound was being piped through a busted kazoo. I loved it.

The doorbell chimed again. "The door!" my father yelled. He was a conservative man who didn't believe in credit, purchased only used cars, and doled out words as stingily as twenty dollar bills. A definite article and noun would suffice for almost any situation.

My mother screamed back from the kitchen, "I am only ONE PERSON!" When I wasn't playing video games, I often puzzled over the philosophical meaning of this statement. Weren't we all just one person? Of course I knew what she really meant: that she was cooking a twenty pound turkey, stuffing, mashed potatoes, green beans, Brussel sprouts, cranberry sauce and pumpkin pie while simultaneously curling her hair and so, no, as a matter of fact, she couldn't answer the door.

I maneuvered Mario onto an innocent-looking sewer pipe where he was quickly devoured by a Venus fly trap. Game over. I looked at the sweaters on my bed. My mother had laid out two: one spangled with elves, the other ducks. Nowadays you might classify this kind of sweater as retro preppy, or hipster ironic, but in 1989 it was only deeply embarrassing.

I pulled on the mallards and entered the upstairs hall. My brother and sister were in their rooms, doors shut as if against a plague.

On this day of coming together and giving thanks, our family didn't seem very interested in coming together or giving thanks. It had been a difficult year. My sister had decided to take a job in Princeton, New Jersey, dashing everyone's hopes of her moving home permanently to Michigan. My brother, who, at thirty, seemed fated to live with us forever, blasting White Snake at high volume and doing bicep curls on the front lawn, had recently met someone and moved in with her. I felt adrift, alone. My parents had begun to drink and fight a lot and I thought it was all my fault. I'd stunned my mother by quitting tennis that summer. In the aftermath, my father decided I should play his sport, baseball. I had no talent. I swung the bat spasmodically, like a deranged samurai warrior. I hit the ball once and ran up the third base line before turning around and being tagged out at home. People on the sidelines pointed and laughed. My father watched alone, in his car. When I told him I was quitting he only peered at me over his newspaper, then went back to reading.

That fall, my mother entered Alcoholics Anonymous, which helped her get sober. It also introduced her to new friends, one of whom she'd invited to Thanksgiving dinner. "You'll love him," she'd told us the day before. "Of course, he has had some problems in his life—"

"The bottle," my father interrupted, clarifying this remark by putting his thumb to his lips as if to drink.

"—but he just needs some cheering up," my mother continued. "He's divorcing and, well, we don't need to mention that. Let's treat him like, you know, family."

My brother and sister and l exchanged glances as that last word stumbled through the room.

Now, I took a deep breath and opened the front door. A man stood on our porch wearing no coat, only layers of sweaters, about four of them. The top-most, ripped and tattered, featured prancing reindeer under a crescent moon. He had a prominent brow, a thick beard and long, greasy hair that fell to his shoulders. If it had been

Halloween I would have put a Snickers in his hand and said, "Let me guess—a Neanderthal!"

Instead, in an oddly soft voice, he introduced himself as John. I let him in and quickly sprinted upstairs and burst into my brother's room.

"Mom's friend is here," I said. "He looks like a caveman. Come quick!"

Soon, we were all seated at the dining room table, listening to each other chew. The silence was excruciating—and strange. Rather than feel embarrassed for this man, I was embarrassed for my own family. His mere presence seemed to expose our dysfunction, our inability to communicate with each other.

"So, John" my father said at last. "Diana tells me you're going through a divorce."

My brother's fork clattered on the floor (no accident) and he excused himself to fetch a replacement. I did the same and then my sister followed. The three of us huddled in the kitchen.

"He's kind of cute," my sister said, "you know, in a primitive sort of way."

"He's definitely primitive," my brother said. "That is, aside from the reindeer sweater."

He slapped me on the back. "Mighty charitable to lend him one of yours."

"I hate this sweater! Mom made me wear it."

My siblings stared at me, as if to state the obvious: that I was fourteen and should probably start dressing myself. "Here's a theory," my brother said. "Maybe he's the Missing Link. You know, like from the movie?"

I remembered. We'd rented it months earlier, just before things got weird in my family. The only character was a pre-lingual man-ape, the last of a fictional species that's been exterminated by early homo sapiens. Fittingly, it was a silent film.

My brother was poking me in the ribs. "What do you think he benches, huh? Two fifty? Three hundred?"

I looked at my brother—suddenly I didn't recognize him. Then I understood: he'd grown a mustache. "When did you grow a mustache?"

"I don't know, a month ago?"

I wasn't sure what was worse, that I hadn't seen him in a month or that neither of us realized it until now. I wanted to crawl under the kitchen table and never come out. I might have, in fact, had I not heard an odd, vaguely familiar noise.

The three of us moved in a kind of hypnotized trance back toward the dining room where the sound grew louder and more distinct. It came from my parents. They were laughing. Together. Stranger yet, my father had left his spot at the head of the table and taken my seat, adjacent to my mother. John was in the middle of a story—something about the cat his wife seized in the divorce—and he had my parents in stitches. I sat down and watched my parents, watched them as if they were new exhibits in a zoo I'd been to a thousand times.

When the story was over my father pushed back his chair but I said it was ok, we could switch places. I passed him his plate and he passed me mine. John told a few more stories, then asked us for some. I told one. So did my sister. John said he'd heard I was a tennis player. I blushed at that and mumbled into my lap about taking some time off. I glanced up and met my mother's gaze—full of pride and love—and I knew then that none of it was my fault. It's ok, she seemed to say. It will be ok.

At Christmas that year, the last present I opened was a new video game system. It had revolutionary features like diagonal movement and stereo sound. Its flagship character was a hyper-active hedgehog, far cooler than Nintendo's plumber whose mustache now reminded me of my brother. I carried the box up to my room with a two-liter of Mountain Dew and a bag of Cool

Ranch Doritos. I planned to binge-play until the sun rose in three days and I had to go back to school. When I reached the top step I paused and, after a moment, turned around. I walked down the stairs and crossed the hall into the family room where my father was sitting in his chair, reading the newspaper. I hooked up the console.

Papers rustled. A chair creaked. My father sat on the floor next to me. "The controller," he said.

I handed it to him, and together we played.

WE WISH NO LESS FOR YOU

You have everything
we could not help
but leave behind—
rough-polished charms,
chiseled tools,
baskets and clay cups
in pieces or unbroken
as the day they last were filled.
Raised up on columns
of stone, in a space
like a temple, marked

and enshrined, fragments
hidden from sunlight, sheltered
from dust. A long wall
painted to seem real—
pine woods, foggy meadow,
smoke lifting from fires.
Children frozen
in play, animals tethered—
as if our days were all
the same. Where

are the storms, the petty
arguments? Our old
were inconsiderate,
our daughters obstinate,
our sons sad.

Our teeth fell out,
and there were some of us
nobody liked. Women
could talk too much
or sit unmoving
in too much silence.
We named everything
with sounds your mouths
can't make. We wish

no less for you—a future
you cannot imagine—
colorless strangers in colorless clothes
who will map your buried city,
raise slabs of stone
to slice away wedges of mud.
shine torches on your shattered wheels,
rusted cooking pots and weapons,
with gloved hands wrap your currency
and holy books in muslin to preserve

their mysterious chains of symbols.
They will whisper and sketch,
wonder what you used
this jeweled neckpiece for,
this stiff-limbed tiny woman,
take everything away
to be numbered, raised up
as on altars in the hush of a room
where a long wall is painted
with flood and flame, sky
streaked with silver,
your children crying

THE SUMMER PEOPLE STARTED DYING

August 2009.
We were scared to go outside after J. didn't come home.
Remembered how his hunted body molded to the pavement of Colby
Street while his spirit
departed
along with the red running from his body like communion wine. We all
became holier,
but without the bullets that hollowed him.
J.'s postered face still secluded on the utility pole molting from the
weather
begging for someone to name who ambushed J. 11 years ago
Grandma would say, "give time, time."

From my childhood, my bus buddies taught me how to cuss,
how to play the dozens, and even later how to drink
The first girl who knew my secrets in high school
Placed a rope around her neck to find relief

The next year, #3 was diagnosed with cancer at 12
We watched her wither away
Her funeral the first place I drove to by myself

When I went to math class #9 wasn't there but the guidance counselor
was
With the sympathy flower
I still thought he was skipping class
His asthma attack solidified his rest
#13, #14, and #15—my bus buddies—all overdosed within a month of
each other. Heroin
#17 worked late hours trying to save others she fell asleep
wrapped herself around a tree

Mama told me of #22 over stale Frosted Flakes
"When you get as old as me," Grandma told me, "memory is all you
have"
I'm experiencing that now

That same evening, I found out about the accident on 74 where #23's
head popped off like a Pez
dispenser after that drunk driver wanted to play Russian roulette

2017, after graduation,
I said I love you and for you to wash your dishes before your flight
I didn't get to hug you
Beside the soiled coffee pot and your 2-bites- removed-everything bagel
your chipped teal coffee mug sat in the sink
2 months and 13 days
Until I could touch it
After the balloon in your chest
Damaged and deflated——couldn't be repaired
Couldn't handle this life anymore
You became #37

Your mother, my grandmother and namesake passed
5 months later—never knowing of your death.

Her mind couldn't recognize how time works within this realm.
She never would've processed her baby boy being gone.
I know I haven't.
She never forgot "I love you." We cared for her until the end.

Romans 8:18 and meds worked only for so long
Here I am hoarding these death dates and death numbers—
A collection I never wanted.
After the 34th...I should've stopped counting

REVELATION

HER mother named her Margaret, but the name slid off the infant's greasy, vernix-coated skin. Everyone who loved the child called her Sweet One.

Sweet One's childhood was the rippling hush of barley in a field, the bubbling of a heavy pot of soup swaying over a fire. It was the flight of a swift almost too high to see, the whiplash of a sapling in a storm. It was fluffy acorn flour, the tickle of a whisper in an ear, the reassuring rhythm of knees bent, straightened, and bent again in prayer.

Sweet One's childhood was the routine, agonized screams of neighbor women in their late hours of labor. It was burials for infants on shimmering summer days. It was funeral masses for mothers held in cold so bitter that Sweet One's fingers blued. It was the choking worry when her own mother's stomach started to swell.

"Sweet One," her mother said, "Have faith. Life finds its way through love."

Sweet One twisted a lock of hair, bit her lip. Alone in the forest, she climbed into the embrace of a sprawling beech, stayed until she could again hold air in her aching lungs.

A stranger arrived asking for Margaret. Sweet One's parents, reluctant but poor, made a deal. There was a wedding feast, and Sweet One lost feeling everywhere except her racing heart. She thought of all the sorrows that follow weddings, and she hid in a shed with a lonely cricket calling. In darkness she snuck away, under the cover of trees whose exposed roots knew the soles of her feet and pressed back, steering her away from slumbering boars.

Sweet One cut her long hair with a knife. She slipped from her dress and stepped into her older brother's loose clothes. Not a change, but a revelation.

Several days of walking, a monastery on a hill. A knock on a door.
"Yes?" said the abbot.
"My name is Pelagian. I've come to devote my life to God. I have an offering," he said, opening his hands to show a small brass crucifix.
"Brother Pelagian. Please, come in."

His new life was spare, precise, but surrounded and insulated by wealth. It was the hushed moment the abbot drew breath to begin Mass, the resonant snores and stale jokes in the dormitories. The burn of sun on his tonsure as he worked to dig a new garden plot for lavender and thyme. The give of vellum, soft but sturdy under his fingers, gold-leafed illustrations crackling to life under flickering candlelight.

Brother Pelagian's life was the feeling of something finally slotting into place, the miracle of a true calling. It was the melody of the brothers' chanted prayer as an elder struggled through his last breaths, it was the silent drowning of a young boy in the monastery's algae-strewn pond. The ache of the boy's weight in Pelagian's arms long after the mother took the small body.

A stranger arrived to speak to the abbot. The damp winter had carried off the monk who governed a nearby nunnery. The nuns needed a new leader and the abbot, reluctant but greedy, made a deal.

Pelagian prayed as others had, that this bitter cup would pass from him. Like others, he was denied. Pelagian moved into the nunnery where every voice reminded him of his mother and sisters.

His life was giving quiet counsel in thick-stone rooms that chilled, soft blessings touched to foreheads both young and creased. It was poverty and porridge, the begging of resources from the wealthy monastery and the denial of the same. It was laboring in scant fields alongside citizens of the village who pitied the nuns and their monk, outcast from the Church's power.

Early one morning Pelagian came around a hedge and saw a young nun picking blueberries. He did not miss the way she braced one hand on her lower back, the slight nudge of her stomach against the front of her habit. Pelagian feared what would come for this girl, knew all searching eyes would turn to him.

He left the garden and walked alone in the forest for three hours. In the darkness of the ancient oaks, fireflies flickered and vines climbed to heaven. Pelagian returned to the nunnery, dark humus on the soles of his shoes. The bitter cup again before him.

Several days of walking, a monastery on a hill. A knock on a door.
"Yes?" said the abbot.
"A nun is with child," said Pelagian.
No questions were asked. Pelagian's brothers took him a cave, left a paltry supply of barley bread and water. The men rolled a rock into place, the scrape of boulder on sand sealing the tomb.

Pelagian had vellum, ink, and a pen hidden in his robes, and his hands did not shake. He began to write about his deep faith and his tremendous love. Of hurrying bees in lavender, of the fox vixen nestled with her kits beyond the creamery. Of fallow deer in rut, of leaping, sparkling salmon battling the current. Of his lost family, his struggling nuns, and his beloved brothers.

Pelagian wrote knowing that when they found this letter beside this body, he'd be sainted for all the wrong reasons. His long-forgotten name recalled, his life rewritten as one of pious sacrifice, of a dark secret kept rather than a flaring, joyous light immolating a bushel basket.

Brother Pelagian wrote his own record to stand next to theirs, and then he slept in the dark heat of the cave, dreaming of wild boar and the baby yet to be born, of all the inheritors of his passion for an imperfect world.

SOURCE MATERIAL:
Tracy, Larissa, ed. *Women of the Gilte Legende: A Selection of Middle English Saints Lives.* Rochester: D.S. Brewer, 2003.

THE ANNUNCIATION

We lived in a world mostly
unlike the world. We didn't know
the names of any growing thing
amid the marble pillars & porticos
& the obelisk of the angel's
ruffling wings. In the ruins
of the oligarchs' harvesting,
their alpha & omega of greed,
the angel's come to tell us
something like *halleluiah*
but we have no music to compare
it to. Something like *holy holy*
but we look out the building's
window instead, into the blue
we call moonlight when we mean
to say wound. In a previous version
of this poem, I wrote: an angel
is just an animal
with wings. I wrote: an icon
is just a flatness climbing
its way to heaven, but now
I believe whatever image
you take within you deeply
can mend you over time,
will bend even God's messenger
down to the empty earth
to teach us the names of each

greening. Bless its red
flowering mouths that open
for anyone. In this version
we refuse the offered suffering
content with the difficulties
we've managed to gather for
ourselves. Leave the worthy
to their ascent & leave
the remorseful to their repentance.
We say, let God
get up from their creaking
wooden throne & stagger
themselves into the broken
world & teach us to sing. And
to mend while we sing, here
in the dusk & mud.

AFTER THE STORM

We parachute into a new garden,
borders erased, minutes changing size.

Can a frozen Eden be well-watered?
Pond's ice-blind eye staring at a white sky.

Strangers follow the red moon. Grow
and diminish. Nothing plain in the unknown.

No longer visiting, yet they're welcome, we set
a plate at the table for unnamed ghosts and guests.

Remember walking downstairs to hug a book,
to trace it, smell it, read a name? At Yad Vashem

a hand and names in tomes, tombs, no Paradise. At
Berlin's Grunewald Station, track 17, metal plaques

one for each deportation of Berlin Jews, Oct. 1941-
Feb. 1945. None of them to Eden. Names extraneous,

not included. Fifty thousand names too many. They
follow moon and word, strange but not extraneous.

Knowing their names is constancy, not lunacy, syn-
ergy between then and now, holding them a choice.

It is boring, says my 7-year-old, stamping her bare foot.
You're old enough to choose, I say, *but know one million*

and a half were children, just like you, murdered for being
what you are. If we don't remember, who will?

Looking at the spring garden greening outside our kitchen,
I pray. When we leave, she comes along, hair brushed and braided.

ACCEPTANCE

after "When I used to focus on the worries, everybody" by Joanne Kyger

If you ask why I don't fear death, a reason good enough for me
is waiting for the kinship of the sun, the light of late afternoon,

weakened after dangling in the heavens, spilling an undulating
glow thru the branches and fissures in the eaves onto the bluish

veins of my hands. I sit on my porch, sip cold water in Virginia—
all the memories that have left me fulfilled. It's simple enough:

I've come to terms with the demands and luxuries of living
life without knowing. I might lick blood from my finger after a

deep cut and get excited with possibility. I believe in the taste.
I recall it, like when we had sex after the movie in my old Buick.

That was some night we had. You were nervous people would
walk by and see us, but they didn't and we did it again, slow and

precise till dawn. Back then I worried over everything I was told
I should want. But now, the trees swaying in the breeze is good

enough for me — it feels like the weekend will be a warm one.
Back then I was taught some vague notion about embracing God,

the best part of dying. The truth? I never knew how insignificant
I was, the ways in which myths were used to make sense of what

we were afraid to lose. Today I wander thru archives of memory,
comfortable among the beautiful trees. Years from now, I hope

I remember them as they were. To be sure, I swear I'll be careful
with my dreams — my time of worrying will be done. I'll taste

blood with my eyes shut tight and let the fragments I've retained
cohere into something worth calling a miracle. I'll trade light

for darkness to learn the magic between the spaces of subtlety—
and so it will end as I pass on into a room of my own choosing.

SURPRISE PARTY

A GIFT of the liberal policies of the Dukakis years permitted my mother, recovering from addiction, to receive training as a nurse. Many mornings she stood before the mirror in her bedroom, adjusting her white outfit against her shoulders, applying her blush, singing old Elvis songs to herself, loving the promise of what she had painstakingly worked herself into becoming.

She had spent just enough time outside of society to view it wryly. Her addiction had required intervention, but it had not been so protracted that it deadened her sense of humor. I never understood why we watched the evening news only for her to hurl invective at the classically appointed Walter Cronkite, whom she hated with a fervor that bordered on derangement; nor did I understand why she remained smitten by the brash and opinionated sportscaster Howard Cosell. Yet this was how she carried herself, and how she computed her private calculus of loves and hates.

I was fourteen when my mother sat at the kitchen table, parsing the magician's cups and balls, her amber hair now fully past her shoulders, intricately curled at its tips:

"Now pay attention," she said, placing a puff ball under a little cup. "It would be better if a father taught you this trick, but then, it would be better if cows had eight udders, too, and if America were a free country."

I watched her manipulating the cups, observing how the ball shifted position. As with all such routines, on the big reveal, the ball was gone, secreted in her palm. "Where's my father?" I asked. I had already heard her response dozens of times, though I noted carefully when a variation crept in.

"Honey, if I could answer you that, I would be the next messiah." She sighed darkly and folded her hands like origami cranes into her lap. "His whereabouts are known but to God."

"I wish I could show him our tricks," I said.

"He would have liked that very much, I'm sure." Once again she manipulated the cups—once again the ball should have been under the center—once again the ball had disappeared.

In the weeks to come, I myself tried to learn the routine. I demonstrated it to her at the end of each day—and at the end of each day, she said the same thing:

"Do it ten thousand times, and it will be yours."

As a teenager in the mid-sixties, she had toured Vietnam. There was a photo in her bedroom of her, much younger, in a glittering tube dress standing among several soldiers somewhere on the edge of a copse of bamboo. Sometimes after a midnight shift at the hospital, she lay in bed late into the morning, and I sat in the chair by her pillow while she stirred, and she spoke to me of that earliest job, of how she had flown Pan American to Vietnam, and how she'd eaten a full meal with a complimentary bottle of wine, and how she'd been given a deck of playing cards *gratis*.

"And that's where you met my father?"

She rolled over in bed so that her back was turned to me. She seemed to be figuring, for reasons that remained out of my reach, and when she took a breath and rolled toward me again, her conclusions remained hidden. "He was a wonderful man," she said poignantly. "A true American hero."

"And he was a warrior?" I asked, though I already knew the answer.

"Noble and full of great virtue," she said. Again, this air of nostalgia. She exhaled deeply. Within herself sat a well spring of torment, touching not only the memory of my father, but some other wound that lay deeper still, that delivered her every Tuesday night to her AA meetings. "I curse that he chose to be a soldier, because sometimes the noblest among us are the first to fall."

I had learned enough from her to see the lineaments of my father: a ghost humping forty pounds of gear through the jungles of Vietnam, brushing leeches from his calves, consigned for all eternity on a perpetual mission to search and destroy. "I'm the child of a hero," I said.

"A man, and every bit a hero. And I see the same heroism, the same marvel, every time I look at you." She smiled wanly as she rose from the bed. She was still wearing her nurses' outfit, and she put on her slippers. She was almost out of the room.

"What really happened to him?" I asked.

Stopping short, it required an odd exercise of strength to answer me. "Honey, I wish that I could tell you good news, good things, about what happened to your father. But the world can be a cruel place. Sometimes people can do bad things to other people, and all the while thinking that they are right, and under cover of their prayers, their justifications, they hurt one another in the worst of ways."

In previous iterations, she told me that he'd been shot in a rice paddy. "What do you mean?"

"I mean," and she drifted away now, out of the bedroom, away from my inquisitions, her voice returning to its crispness, to the comfort of certainty. "I mean that Vietnam was a hell storm, and some people never came home."

SOMETIMES she stumbled, and she had to be careful, and sometimes in the morning it was as though she had been crying. This life was so much different from what she had promised herself when she was a girl. I knew that however much I might offer her, I could only ever be her son. Some children are wanted more, and some children are wanted less. I had sensed that from birth.

Sometimes she would return from her AA meeting and go upstairs straight to bed, and she would fall asleep with her clothes on, the tension seeping out of her into the darkness. And other times I would curl up on the sofa, and she would, too, and we would watch television right up until it was time for me to sleep. She was beautiful, and she lived like a nun. Even as I lived with her, watched her perform it every day, I failed to understand the precariousness of her high wire act. Nor did I understand how much of her hurt was my father's doing—and beyond that, how much of it was America's to bear.

I love this country and I hate it, too. Anyone truly patriotic— anyone who has pledged allegiance on an empty stomach in white-knuckled fatherless mourning—will know exactly what I mean.

I STILL remember that it was spring, perhaps a month later, when she stood upright in the kitchen and lectured me on being a man. She leaned forward to gesture, a ladle gripped tight in her fist, the dirty linoleum squeaking underfoot.

"You will learn showmanship. It is important to be able to stand on your feet and charm a crowd. If you want to get somewhere in life, you should have a little flair."

"Ok."

"That was what your father was like."

"He was a showman?"

"He was a *manipulator*. He manipulated me. You don't think he did?"

"I don't know."

"He played me like a regular glass armonica," she said. "That's what this world is. We don't worry about eating anymore, or feeding. But you still have to figure out how to keep somebody else under your thumb if you want to get somewhere. And you'll keep a lot of people under your thumb if you want to get rich."

"I don't want to live like that."

She laughed sardonically. "*Everybody* lives like that. We live in the greatest country in the world with the greatest system in the

127

world. That's capitalism. And some day you'll meet a nice girl and you'll hold her heart in your hand. And then someday, you'll tell her about yourself, you'll share with her what you feel, and you'll stay with her whatever the weather, and you'll be an honorable man, and you'll build a life with her. And you'll make her do whatever you say, but you'll treat her well, too, because that's how it works between a man and a woman, and in a capitalist society, too."

"What happened with my dad?"

"Sweetie, maybe I'm not fair to him. But your father was never the same after Vietnam. And now he's gone."

"He made it home from Vietnam?"

She rolled her eyes for me, again began calculating. I could see the thoughts like sparrows flickering across her face. "He died there," she said hurriedly. "His bones were never recovered."

"But you just said —"

"Sweetie, you'll never see him topside again."

"But you just said —"

"He should be forever gone from your heart."

She'd had enough. Waving me off, inured to my entreaty, she went upstairs to her bedroom and closed the door.

IT was a summer derecho, the wind speeding up without warning, rifling empty trash barrels down the road, knifing through the trees, their leaves a tattered wedding dress. Years later I remember it as historic, the Derecho of '86, though no one else I've ever met has the least recollection of it. But it was a day later, in the wake of the wind—with the municipality clearing limbs from roads, stacking cordwood on the sidewalks, and the power company frantic with bucket loaders, restoring lines all up and down the lanes—that along came the second derecho, who strode right up to our front door in his crimson dungarees and loose plaid shirt and pushed the bell twice and, when I answered, wryly introduced himself.

"I must be your father," he said.

"What?"

"Looks like it's the truth," he said.

He was not what I imagined. He was two inches shorter than me, and he had a limp and a lazy eye. In those ways we differed. Yet on closer inspection, his was the face that stared back at me from the mirror, albeit twenty-odd years more advanced—the same elongated, almost equine jaw, the same nostrils like the entrance to a cave, the same disappearing upper lip. We had the same wispy peanut-colored mop, the same hairline like a seagull floating in the wind.

He had a familiar way of smiling. It was uncanny until I realized that his smile, too, was my own.

"I thought you were dead," I said, and I opened the door to let him in.

"She told you that?" He shook his head, but then he laughed easily, and even his laugh was my own. "That's not right. Even if I haven't ever come by, that's still not right."

My mother walked down the stairs. I might have expected an outburst, but she remained lucid, uninflected. "It isn't far from the truth," she said, and the hardness in her voice signaled to me that she had been anticipating this visit, if not so much for hours, then for years.

"Technically so, but it also isn't true," he said. He took a flask from his back pocket and gestured up to her with it. She shook her head. "My blood is still pumping!"

"Vietnam might as well have killed you."

"But it didn't," he said fiercely. "I have concluded, in fact, that it was Vietnam where I learned how to live." He drank from his flask.

"Alright, I'm going to bite my tongue," she said, and she addressed me almost plaintively. "My dear," she said to me, "this is your father. I wish I could have told you before now, but I didn't think that you would ever see him."

"You're seeing me now!"

She groaned.

Much in the way that after you fall on the ground, it takes a full minute before your knee cap really lets you know how badly you're damaged, it would be a lie to say that I even knew what I felt, beyond that I was keenly alive, and that this man was standing firmly, unimpeachably before me. I was discomfited by his presence, his smoldering aura. I didn't know if I should laugh or weep.

"I want to take you some place special," he said, turning on me, and again I noted the similarity of his vanishing upper lip to my own. "Can I?" he asked irrelevantly. "Where's a playground?"

"There's a playground at the school," I said. "It's a five-minute walk from here."

"Jeepers! Let's go!"

"I'm too old for playgrounds," I said. "I'm fourteen."

"Nonsense. Are you too old for fun?"

"No sir," I said.

"Then we're going to the playground!" He bounded down the steps into the sunlight. He stood waiting for me beside a little pile of sticks that had become snaggled by the derecho on the edge of the front yard. "Come on!"

"I'll be here," my mother said bluntly.

I came out the front door, and my father let out a little laugh, and we walked together toward the school. It was an easy walk, and half way there, he took a pack of Marlboros from his back pocket and held them up to me. "You want one?" he asked.

"No, thank you. I don't smoke."

"Wow, you're shiny!" He got a far-away look, then added quickly: "And you don't drink either, I hope?"

"No sir," I said.

"Shiny and clean!" He lit a cigarette.

It was a dilapidated, really shitty little playground, made more so by the derecho, which had knocked the sign in the entrance off its moorings. The swings were tangled and dangling, and the monkey bars were too low to the ground. The slide was cracked at the bottom, liable to tear someone's pants. I hadn't used the playground in years. My father ran toward the sandbox, the cigarette bobbing from his lower lip. "I love playgrounds!" he hooted. "Look over here. You want to go down the slide with me?"

"Dad, I'm too big for the slide."

"Alright. Well, *I'm* not too big for the slide," he said, and he scrambled up the ladder and perched on the top. He slid down faster than anticipated and landed square on his butt, and the ash from his cigarette skittered into his lap.

"Ouch," he said. He got up, rubbing his legs. "I won't do that again. You want me to push you on the swing?"

"I'm a little big for that, too."

He stepped onto the swing and stood upright, holding the chains on either side. He began to sway back and forth, fully upright. The swing set was rusty and it groaned under his weight.

"What're you doing so big?"

"It happens. She feeds me well."

"You're going to be a giant," he said, marvelling.

He was swinging hard in his upright position, and I was concerned that he would lose his grip and fall backwards in mid-air. At last, he grew tired and allowed the swing to return to a more normal cadence, and thereafter he leapt from it, landing with a few stumbles but remaining more or less upright, surprisingly spry. I really didn't know how old he was. His cigarette tumbled to the ground and sat burning in the sand. "World's biggest ash tray," he said, laughing again, now with a smoker's ack-ack sound. He reached into his pocket. "Look here, take this." He handed me a quarter.

I didn't know what to do with it, so I made a fist and held it tight. "Thank you," I said.

"But look at it," my father said, gesturing. "The money's not the point. Look!"

I obeyed him. The quarter was typical, George Washington in bas relief.

"You see?" he said proudly. "That's the father of our country. I thought when I came, what if I gave you a thousand dollars? But I didn't want to cheapen you with money. Because money is just money. It's not a message. A boy has a father, and he wants to have a message. So I wanted to leave you with wisdom, and that wisdom is all right here, in this man's unfurrowed brow."

"We studied Washington in school. The Cincinnatus of the West."

"I'm sure you did. Cherry tree and all. This is the greatest country in the world, and don't ever let anyone tell you otherwise. A man can be his own man in this country. I've been in the tundra and the desert, and the high mountains and the plains, and the lakes and the oceanside, and I've been hiking through thick pines and into squid black mine shafts, and sometimes, I'm not ashamed to say, I've slept in alleys, and on forgotten mattresses putrifying with mold, and I've slept in abandoned cars, or cars that were soon to be abandoned, and through it all, I've always thanked God that I was born an American, the greatest land on earth. That's what I mean to tell you." He exhaled after his speech, because it had taken effort from him, and he had delivered it with a bold sincerity, so that I understood that he believed deeply, or at least wanted to. He took the flask from his back pocket and stole a swig, offering it to me insincerely, returning it to his pocket, and then we walked together out of the playground, angling again toward home.

He strode fondly beside me, neither fast nor slow. For all his flaws, he was my father, and for so long I hadn't dared to believe that he existed still. I felt within myself an upwelling of love.

"Why didn't you come before?" I asked, because among all the other questions, this was the one that I most wanted him to answer. He ignored it.

"You have your mother's eyes," he said. "Do you have your mother's tears, too?"

"Sir?"

"Of course you do," he said off-handedly. We walked the remainder of the way in silence until we reached the house, and we stood outside by the doorway. "Ok. You're a great boy, and I've got to be going soon, but I am so very glad to finally meet you." He bowed to me and performed a theatrical flourish.

"But where do you live?"

"Houses are for suckers," he said. "Man is born free but everywhere he is in chains. You get it?"

"I get it."

We went inside. My mother was waiting for us, ringing out a dish towel until her hands were blotchy.

"Life means nothing—*nothing*—if you are not free to be you and me," he said aloud, no longer just to me but also, it seemed, to my mother.

"But why now?" I asked. Too late I realized that the question sounded different in front of my mother—that it was a booby trap. His expression flittered darkly, and then he was himself again.

"Shouldn't I have come a long time ago?" he answered.

"Yes," said my mother. "You should have."

He looked to my mother. "Do you mind if I smoke?"

"You can do what you like, I could never stop you."

He lit up and puffed out an easy blue mist.

"How about you join me?" he asked her. "It's been too long."

"I can't believe you're saying that," she said.

"Ok, that's not what I meant," he said hurriedly.

"I can't believe you," she said.

"You never could. Yet here I am." Again he exhaled, and the smoke filled the foyer and mixed about the ceiling.

She turned away from him.

"You're still young," he said.

"That has nothing to do with it."

"I've come to talk with you about the boy, and for you to open a path to me. That's why I'm here. And I have things to say to you. Why do you deny me?"

"I don't," she said neutrally.

"When did I ever lie to you?"

"Wrong question."

"I mean about something important. And now I'm asking you." He held his hand out imploringly. He dropped down on one knee. "I'm asking you." He was abasing himself, his head hung low.

Absently she touched her hair. "Alright," she said mildly. "If that's what this is about. I'll go with you if you refrain from embarrassing yourself."

"Alright then," he said. He stood up again.

"Alright," she said again more firmly. "Alright." She grabbed her purse.

"God is smiling on me today," he mused. He grinned beautifully. "You'll need to bring the cash because I'm kind of light right now."

"Alright," she said, shrugging. "Honey, don't stay up too late, alright?"

"I won't," I said.

"That's my boy," she said.

"And a fine job you've done," he said. "We had what I can only characterize as a really special, really important time at the playground, and I don't want to presume except to say that I had a lot of things that I needed to say to him, and I think, if I'm not wrong, son, that you heard me say them?"

I nodded obliquely.

"This may be the happiest day of my life," he added.

"I'll be back soon, honey," she said.

"Alright," I said.

"But not too soon, I hope," said my father, and he winked at me conspiratorially, and because he was my father, and because I was stunned, and because I was hungry, I winked back at him, though I didn't even know why.

When they were out of earshot and beside the road, my father gestured widely at the expanse of sky before him. He had no car, so they walked back down the driveway and got into my mother's little compact. She drove them out of the driveway and took a left, in the direction of the highway that would take them into Boston.

I went to sleep that night without seeing her. When I woke the next morning, she still wasn't home.

All told, she didn't come back until the morning of the day thereafter. And when she did come back, she was alone, and her eyes had guttered, and there was a rug burn on her chin and there were needle tracks were on her arms.

IT is strange at that age to see a parent fail. Strange at any age, really, but in the teenage years, everything is a potential mortification, and the failure of a parent emphatically so. Even as I was embarrassed for myself—a teenage reaction—I also regretted my own selfishness for feeling embarrassed, and thus layered guilt on top of worry, and sorrow on top of guilt. Those of us who have been through such things will recognize the contradictions, the muddiness—the way the shame stays with you, how the cocktail of humiliation and dirtied love even years later rises like bile to the throat.

She came home with a rug burn on her chin, and she called in sick to work. She called in sick the day after that, as well, and she remained in bed for much of the coming week. During waking hours, she seemingly did not leave the home—at least, I never saw her out of bed. I would go out into the world—mostly to school — and I would come back to find her in her bed, except that by some act of stealth, she would be wearing clothes where before she had been in underwear, or she would be in underwear instead of clothes, and as often as not she would be blissed out in an addled haze. In the mornings when I departed, she would be dead asleep and wouldn't rise until the afternoon, after I'd come home, but then at five a.m., I might wake to a noise, and I would go to her room and find her again in her bed, wide-eyed, covered in smears of her own make up, her elbows worn raw and her fists slicked with her own tears. I knew then that she had to be leaving at strange hours, but by her own design I never caught her at it, which I think was the last vestiges of her heroic effort to protect me. For all her apparent languor, her body was not at rest. Her cheeks very quickly became taut and sallow. This pattern persisted for perhaps half a month.

Toward the end, I was able to rouse her early one evening, and my first question was so obvious as to be silly, except that I did not know how else to ask her, to establish the truth of what was plain. Under the covers she was wearing blue jeans and a black Rush t-shirt.

"Did you relapse, mommy?"

She glanced at me lazily, one eye not quite in synch with the other. "No, honey, I'm fine," she said, in a voice thick with exhaustion. "Every day in every way I get better and better."

"What can I do for you?"

She sniffled, ignored my question. "The best thing about heroin was that it kept me thin," she said.

"You're fine, Mom, just like you are."

"No, honey, I'm really not. I'm grossly overweight. But some men like it that way. They think—I don't know what they think. They think they're wolves and that I'm a fat lamb. That's how they think."

"Are you hungry?"

"I should try to keep something down," she said. But her eyes shuttered again, and she was asleep.

I made myself a dinner of peanut butter and jelly sandwiches and Hi-C. I made the same for her. I brought it upstairs to her on a wooden tray. She woke again, shivering, rubbing her arms to get warm.

"You are a wonderful, generous son to cook dinner for your mother," she said, and she ate her way into the peanut butter and jelly sandwich. "Oh honey, I hate it that you see me like this."

"It's alright," I said. It was my duty to say it.

"No, it isn't," she said. "It's just how I am right now."

"I love how you are," I said,—but even now, I wonder if that was a mistake. Do you give them your full support, the entire measure of your love, even as they drive themselves to ruin? Would it be better to withhold? "You are the best mother any son could ever have."

"But don't," she said. And she closed her eyes into a squint. "I want you to break the cycle."

"I'm so proud of you," I said, because again, it seemed like the proper thing to say, even as it was the most sardonic, the most wrong thing of all. She stared at me, and I understood that some distant part of her was afraid for me, for how ill-equipped I was. And then I allowed myself to understand further without reservation, to really understand, that she was collapsing before my eyes, that this would last much longer than a week or two. I had not permitted myself that understanding before, because facing it was to accept the warm-blooded anxiety of being a teenage orphan, cast out to rely upon chance and neighborliness. People do not know how paralyzing it is to dwell in fear.

"I won't begin the cycle," I pledged.

But she was asleep again, a half sandwich beside her on the bed, her brain shut down under a pharmaceutical influence whose power I couldn't fathom—and to this day, mercifully, cannot fathom. I left her room and shut the door behind me. It would have been better if I could have locked it.

I WOULD like to say that I hated my father for bringing us to this. But I could not conjure up a feeling that intense for him. The man I'd met was so far from the father of my dreams that I could not accept him as my father, even while I knew that he had sired me, and knew even better that the forces that my mother contended with were independent of any other person, were themselves a species of weather over which I certainly had no control, to which we could only submit as reluctant victims.

When I woke the next morning, she was out of her bed, with a suitcase packed beside her.

"Honey, I need to go away for a while," she said. "Seeing your father kinda pushed me over the edge. We used to do this together, you know, and it brought it all back."

"Will I see him again?" Within me all was mixed. I wanted to see him again, to yell at him. I wanted to share with him how proud he should be of her — and how well we had done in his absence — and how little we needed him. I wanted to return his quarter.

"He said he'd come back, but I don't think he will."

"He has a way of surprising you," I said.

She shrugged. "Yes, but it's never been happily." She glanced down at her bag. "So I need to check myself into rehab. You deserve better than this. *We* deserve better than this."

"I just want you to be well," I said, and I was bracing myself.

"Ok!" she said.

I helped her carry her bag downstairs. There was already a taxi idling outside. I carried the bag down the front steps, with her weakly swaying behind me. She stood still beside the taxi, like an expectant sparrow, her nose twitching, and she rubbed her cheek with her sleeve.

"I wish I were older," I said.

"You and me both," she said, and she wiped her brow with her sleeve. From behind the wheel, the taxi driver looked at us expectantly. "When you can't stand it, when you really can't, here's a trick I've learned," she said. She let her arms fall limp to her sides. "First, you put on a pair of red shoes, ok? And then you close your eyes and click your heels three times like this."

She demonstrated, but the effort of clicking almost made her stumble against the car. A summer wind blew around her, swaddled her, dragged her hair like corn silk across her face.

A month later I'd be in foster care.

"Now you try it," she said. She moved away from me and opened the taxi door. And then she was in the backseat, facing the road. She tapped the driver on the shoulder.

"Mom?" I said, though already she wouldn't hear me, and the taxi was pulling away, and it bore her down the road into the rising heat of summer.

The hot wind blew upon me. I let my arms fall limp. I closed my eyes, and I clicked my heels three times. "I want to be old," I said. "I want to be old. I want to be old." The light shifted all around me. I braced myself for opening my eyes.

SCOLIOSIS

Each day, my back reminds me
that pain is an artist.

Some mornings, my pain
is a contortionist performing in carnival,

bright fire in its mouth, bending
in ways my body won't.

Some days, a boring lecturer,
the dullest words culled

from an iron alphabet.
A deep-sea diver,

pulling pain like long strands
of seaweed through my spine.

Violetta in La Traviata,
rising to an aria so high

it vibrates in my skin.
Some days, my pain holds

out an olive branch, and when I reach,
retracts it. There are days when my pain is a baker,

kneading and stretching my joints see-through thin.
My pain scatters its numbers across my back until

the scale of one to ten becomes a puzzle,
pieces I can't fit together.

I try once more to learn how to count.

MAKING WAVES

Confession: on days when I feel
very small, I've found a new love
in eavesdropping. On walks,
I often listen in
on the river's conversation
with the rocks, the sandpipers
shouting directions into the cloudless
air as they begin their trip to winter
down on the Georgia coast.
Lately, I have been so quiet
that I've nearly forgotten I exist.
That each name we sing is the name
of eternity, and when we gaze
upon the keen eye of the rabbit,
statuesque if not for the panic of breath,
we are the universe both in awe
of itself and in fear
of what we may do.

BOUND TO HAPPEN

Nearly every soul I know has hit a deer
on this wooded road.
A road so dark you cannot see
even a glimmer of light
in the wall of trees
standing tall along the way.

One day our turn will come.
A deer will slide from the woods
to the asphalt like a shadow,
so quickly that you, my dear,
will see too late.

Would it not be agreeable,
to slow our fast car down,
nose our fender into the grasses
growing lush along the roadside,
where we could curl beside each other
and watch the moon rise
and the deer come and go,
their hearts still beating
in their precious chests.

We could talk fondly till dawn
of old times, old hurts and scars.
We could forgive each other
everything and pretend

we have not neared the end,
but have only stopped midway
on our journey across a great
green continent. Oh, yes,

it would be agreeable,
but you do not stop.
You drive on.
Toward home, you say,
we must return home.
You even claim
to know the way.

KILLING THE BUDDHA AND EATING HIM

"Your mind is a nightmare that has been eating you: now eat your mind."
                                            -Kathy Acker

THE summer was feral. Slusarz was in town, and we went with Matt to meet a dealer halfway and pick up ten grams of mushrooms. When we went back to Matt's place we sat beneath an umbrella beside the backyard pool, snug in the mid-August heat where we ate the Penis Envy and watched the clouds billowing cotton through the pale wide ascending blue and the wind that we couldn't see moving through the thickly green branches of the trees beyond the fence, the water of the pool clear and lapping and rippling with the gentle but firm breeze. A few weeks earlier I'd had a ketamine infusion, a tune-up following a breakdown in Tulsa, some five months or so after my second round of treatment with tablets. During those sessions I made a lot of progress. I slowly began to learn how to detach thoughts from feelings, to center myself in a space between emotion and reason; I began to feel the capacity for self-love that had been for so long full of rotten emptiness. There had been an encounter with an entity that my mind labeled "god" despite my materialist/atheist mindset, and there had been experiences with pure and joyful gratitude and appreciation for life and all its workings. In a doctor's office with a needle sticking from my hand, I cried out of joy and relief for the first time in my life. These experiences had opened me up to a remaining potential for recovery despite the stalled feeling I'd been having; the intravenous tune-up in July of 2022 gave me the boost I needed to push past some uncomfortable events and maintain a grip on a sobriety that could only be regarded as tenuous.

Ketamine and mushrooms produce very different varieties of hallucination (while LSD is a whole different beast altogether), and although I *have* used psilocybin in a recreational setting (Lionel Richie had three mouths), I don't recommend treating either substance as anything other than medicine—considering their potential for psychological healing and change, they are weighty chemicals that should not be regarded lightly, while also standing importantly and quite clearly apart from mere "drugs." Think of them as lenses. The former is considerably shorter in duration (one hour compared to four or five), but sometimes stronger in effect; ketamine opened the curtains shading some of the windows in my mind that I hadn't the capacity to open myself—it comes on like an internal wave, or like dropping gradually into a current that is usually inaccessible to oneself, fastmoving and clear and rich with the calmly ineffable; psilocybin, on the other hand, crawls over its subject from the inside out like an interdimensional mold, and once it has taken a fusing grip to you, you are in its thrall and there is nowhere to disappear to but everywhere at once. Both ketamine and psilocybin deserve bits of credit for facilitating my recovery from both addiction and mental illness; they provide the temporary flexibility necessary to begin working important cognitive muscles—the exercising of fingers fine enough of tissue and bone to dig into the cleaves in knots of thought and unravel them like coiled parasites wrapped up in the mind; malleability is a choice that is not always made willingly, and sometimes even when the will is there, it's not enough. Sometimes a shock to the system is needed, an attack not simply on the structure but on the foundation of the Self as one perceives and presents it.

That day the dose had to be somewhere around an eighth each—we didn't weigh the dried caps and stems, eyeballing amounts in our sweaty palms. It came on slow. Matt, Slusarz and I watched the water until it began to shimmer like a big puddle of sky, and we waded in and spun and dipped through the cool clear blue as our movements further undulated and lapped the water at the edges of what had begun to seem like the membrane of a cell, the three of us bounding back and forth in a vat of cytoplasm; we swam and watched the trees which began just beyond the fence, their canopies crawling in the temperate wind that pulled sideways over the earth in gusts that I began to feel the atmospheric height of as I bobbed in the weightless chlorine jelly, cool and blue. Beginning to lose my sense of different kinds of matter (air and water, for instance), I swam to the concrete wall of the pool and hung onto the lip of it. Slusarz looked at me and I gazed back and through them, and I made a confused face and said

—Dogs with . . . human feet?

It was not long afterwards that we decided that getting out of the pool was a good idea.

We sat in patio chairs, wrapped in beach towels and dripping wet shadows onto the concrete. As we sat, smoked, and talked, I gradually grew quiet—my friends were under the impression that I was just in a daze, and in a sense, they were right—what I could not communicate was that my sense of the meaning of words had detached itself from the sound of them. I could recall simple phrases or clusters of words, standard responses, and conversational niceties, but I had no clue what any of it meant, and so I went mute. It was in this silence, this absence of language, that I began to see the web of Being begin to stretch out in front of me like a nervous system growing itself out in its multitudinous spindles and branches and weavings of gossamer and foliage, hair and blood. Every living thing—plant, mammal, insect, parasite, Water Bear—presented itself before me as a leaf on a humungous tree; this sense of connectedness was utter and whole. I immediately lost all grip on history, social norms, and cultural contexts, and what I thought of as my Self no longer had any borders, or if it did then they were porous—I felt a deep, familiar understanding of other creatures flow through me, and I found myself to be inseparable from the whole of Being as time dilated past its borders, and I suddenly became unsure if I'd been alive for thousands of years, or simply decades; space became just more air to move through on the nervous circuit, and I found myself somewhere in Southeast China for a few moments, pinballing through spacetime as—with time and space having grown malleable if not inconsequential—I began to remember the concept of Death. I looked down at my tendril veils standing out clear through my cool pale gooseflesh and I began to realize that I had drowned; perhaps all three of us had. I panicked; I stood and quickly changed still dripping into my clothes before fleeing Matt's backyard and wandering out into the neighborhood; the sun was slowly going down and I knew I had to go somewhere, and so I decided to follow the sun since that was a sentiment that I remembered. After maybe five minutes of this, something in me clicked, and I began to do a beeline back to my house, wandering with a mind wiped of any semblance of Self—a puppet skittering automatically towards some instinct of safety—stopping only once to examine a neighbor's mailbox with genuine curiosity. Believing I was dead, my mind had evacuated itself. It was as though I had done a "factory reset," to put it one way; I could not recall any information whatsoever, moving and acting on instinct and muscle memory alone.

The rest of the night and into the following day was a prolonged exercise in rediscovery—I remember walking up to the microwave and being unsure how it worked, and deciding to just let my hands move and push buttons with the confidence that it would come back, and it did. I remember being guided through a grocery store by Slusarz as I marveled at my rediscovery of the distinction and diversity of life and matter, beginning to ground my under-standing that there are discreet things in the world (like apples or bread or Pringles) and expressing this as—Look at just how many different *things* there really are! And every one of them has a *name*! while Slusarz wondered if I needed to be taken to the hospital. I remember asking my friends questions about my life the next morning, still fully amnesiac, and being confused at their confusion when I asked them if I was a good person:

—We can't tell you that, they said.

I respect that answer.

After maybe thirty-six hours, when I'd recovered enough to convey any of this in a way that made sense, I felt as though I'd shed something. I'd relearned what words like "depression" and "paranoia" meant, but I could not relate to them, could not find any part of myself that identified with them; of course, this didn't last, but for several days to a week I felt a quietly strong elation glowing through my life. While this nearly overwhelming aura of joy, gratitude, and calm awe eventually subsided, I retained its roots, the knots and curls and trestles of the sort of Being that even in my grimmest days of illness I knew was buried beneath a thick mantle of scar tissue through which these coils of light now threaded to brace me as I bent to the work of healing myself, of picking back the calloused dead flesh with my thumbnail in a pinch and digging through the dead-matter that I had massed around my heart under the guise of muscle. It took another year of dialectical behavioral therapy, medication adjustments, white knuckling, night drives, sweats cold and hot, irresponsible amounts of coffee and nicotine, and six more variations of the ego death experience to drag me fully into recovery. As of now I'm laying off psychedelics indefinitely.

The occasions of "dying" that I experienced between my first ego death and the last were in equal measure profound, terrifying, and transformative; my wife has seen pictures of me from the days before my first brush with ego death and from the days immediately following, and she says she can see a difference in my eyes.

— They're darker, before, she says.

Maybe it's the lighting, but she isn't wrong.

The last time that I experienced ego death, she was there with me; I meant to take a light dose, but as I was subsumed into the mushroom haze, I forgot what the little dried pieces were and found myself idly munching through the rest of the eighth. By the time I realized what was happening, it was too late to do anything but prepare her for it.

—I'll likely lose the ability to speak, and I might not know where or who I am, I said. —I might get confused or scared. This has all happened before, though; I know how to navigate this and I'll be OK.

I managed these words as I simultaneously found it more difficult to move my mouth. For the next three hours I drifted in and out of fugues of Self; I remember watching a childhood memory unfold in a litany of variations as though I were watching alternate universes play out—I remember losing everything my mind tried to hold onto; just as before, history and biography ran through and out of my mind like it was a broken sieve. I remember becoming overwhelmed with horror, clenching my right index finger with my teeth and feeling almost unable to keep my eyes open, growing gradually convinced that I had bitten my finger off and bled to death. I remember thinking that my then-fiancé would abandon me after bearing witness to the mad circuitry of my mind. I remember her folding her arms around me and bringing me back to rest against her as my eyes turned to the roof, the thunder rustling there above us, and lightning flicked white through the high-ceilinged windows of that boxy warehouse apartment. I remember growing peacefully unsure, as she held me, where she ended and I began.

I never forgot who she was.

A DREAM

Where the snow blinding, white lay cross the fields so thick and
deep
we could step thigh high into a drift and the sharp red glint
of a redbird's wing flashed above our bowed heads.
Or while jogging up the mountain road one night during spring
thaw,
our eyes barely perceived that dark place at roadside
where a grizzly shebear spied our footfall from the shadows.
Up the mountain path to our cabin nestled on a hillside
where all the simple dreams of life came true.
On the woodstove fire a kettle warmed to a shrill whistle
while the wind circled tornados among the leaves.
And where we watched, very still, through the open doorway
as the black shebear crouched on hind legs beside the creek
teeming
        with trout
scooped out the helpless fish its blue gills trembling with death.
Where you stripped me naked in the chill,
wrapped my shivering body in your heavy lumberjack shirt
and a ragged flannel blanket. Too frozen to make love
we brewed tea. Cracked teacups filled with Earl Grey,
the comfort of warm liquid spilled onto our china saucers.
Our souls came to reside in those woods:
to grapple in the silence of growing things –
the trees added each a year to our own brief lives.
Where no one knew what secret we were withholding
from those below in the valley more broken who dared not dream.
Where we huddled together in the night beyond speaking.

CONVERSATIONS WITH MY SON

You tell me the Age of Fear begins that magic year – 1978:
same year your daddy parades around Greenwich Village
singing and dancing his own dark musical poems.
Your daughter is four. Sees in you that same dark magic.

There is a certain stillness about you tonight. A tough calm.

I hear your voice hovering over the distance between us.
Now the distance is my age measured by all these humble years,
the time of certain decline, cataracts like pearls in my eyes, slow
limping of gait.
Your daughter has learned to count numbers,
to spell with her private alphabet.
Numbers no longer matter to me now,
as if age is just another word for tired, so tired.

You forgave the years of pain: trauma, love and lies.
Did your daddy ever really love me?
Did he ever really love himself?

And you, my son, at age forty-seven, steps forward
accepting all the worship due a grown man with your kind of
wisdom.

You say it is the Fear, brought on by time,
ravaging all within us like a heartache.

—Bryana Joy—

POEM FOR WHICHEVER OF US IS LEFT

I know how cold Comfort is I know
you have no interest in getting over it,
in sun or moon anymore, in beginnings.
I did not write this poem to say what
everyone is saying, no *oh but you're still
young!*s, no timid *have you thought about
dating again?*s. No agains. I have come
carrying in my hands a gift as gentle as
feathers, as rich as the frail drumming
of a bird's heart. Listen to me dearest.

This in whatever way it came was not
a surprise. Remember how we were
trying to prepare for it in every subway
car and on the airplanes we were often
taking together and apart? The low wail
of this thing was a theme writhing under
all our music. We put our ears next to it,
promised to find each other in any
universe if death isn't the end. Still, we
took no chances, as you know, my
Always friend. This was why we kissed

goodbye each morning at the door no
matter our mood sometimes one time
sometimes kissing and kissing and you

leaving and then running back up the
stairs with your hair wet like ocean
your mouth as delicate as eager as a
swan dive saying one more one more

LOOK OUT

At a look-out just west of the Mosier Tunnels
a herd of tourists admire the view, comment
that the island down there with the white jetty
and a brick house would be a good place to stay.
A $500 a night kinda hotel place. They all nod.

I thought it was the sacred Native burial island,
confusing it with the one upstream. Feeling
displaced justice, I quietly condemn them all
as fattened city day-trippers, electronically
assisted and ignorant. I am the ignorant one.

This is Eighteenmile Island, or locally known
as Chicken Charlie's Island. From 1915-1963,
Charles Reither lived there and died there,
had a chicken ranch / never had chickens.
Truth lost. Now a $500 a night day-dream

THE CELESTIAL DREAMS
OF BUCKIE AND DOT

THE DAY after Caroline found out that Miles died, she quit her job and moved to the desert. People always said don't make any decisions right after a death, but it wasn't exactly a decision. She started doing things and couldn't stop herself. She didn't want to stop herself. There was no wanting or not wanting. She sold all of her furniture and moved out of her apartment right on the river in Portland, Oregon. She rented a U-Haul trailer, crammed her 12-year-old tabby Crumbles into a carrier, settled her messy-haired self behind the wheel, and drove down to Grandma Shipley's abandoned house on the outskirts of Victorville, smack on the edge of the desert.

"You must be happy that the world is rid of him," her sister Mia said when Caroline called her from the road to tell her about Miles. "Is that road noise? Are you driving?"

"Yes, I'm on the road. I'm moving to the desert house. You know, Grandma's house."

"What? What about your job? Can you pull over? I can barely hear you."

"I quit it!" Caroline shouted.

"Why on earth would you do that? And that house is a wreck. I don't even know where the keys are. Do you have them? Why are you going there?"

Caroline thought for a moment. "I don't really know why," she said quietly, then remembered the road noise. "I don't really know why! I just want to! I've been keeping the keys in the back of my sock drawer, remember?!"

"No, I don't remember. You can stop shouting. I can hear you better now. Caroline, I was just thinking the other day that we should sell that house. Nobody's been there in years, and we could use the money. Both of us could. And you're too old for a mid-life crisis."

"We can't sell it!" Caroline said. "I'm going to live there. Mia, I'm barely fifty. And it's not a mid-life crisis. It's the opposite of a crisis."

"You're fifty-three. And what about your life in Portland? I thought you loved it there."

"I did. Now I want to live in the desert. In Grandma's house."

The fact was, after she heard about Miles, Caroline had to go somewhere. Her body started moving around, and then it couldn't stop moving. It couldn't stop cleaning, packing, sorting, then couldn't stop driving, turning on the radio, turning off the radio, pulling into rest areas, checking on Crumbles, pulling out of the rest areas, looking at trees, counting trucks and hawks and Teslas.

It didn't make much sense because the fact was that she and Miles weren't together anymore and hadn't been for ten years, no thirteen years. So she didn't really have a right to feel this bad when Miles died. She knew that. Caroline had been the one to break them up. Mia had told her to leave him for years. Her friends had told her to leave him for years. Miles was mean. Miles drank, and he hit her more than she ever told anyone. Every time he got mean, Caroline imagined herself driving away from San Francisco and going to the desert, to Grandma Shipley's old house near Victorville. Finally she did drive away, but instead of going to the desert, she drove up I5 to Portland, Oregon. She started a new life, there in Portland. Yay Caroline for thirteen years. But then Miles went and died.

Caroline remembered the desert house from her childhood. Grandma Shipley bought the house long before Caroline was born, way back in 1932, when lots of Hollywood people like her were buying cheap houses in the desert. Grandma Shipley worked in scripts, and, according to her, in the 1930s there were script writers, set designers, makeup artists, and sound people, not to mention directors, producers, and actors, scattered across the desert from Palmdale to Borrego Springs.

Caroline drove for two days, stopping over in Red Bluff. Finally, she pulled up to the house with her U-Haul. As soon as they stopped moving, Crumbles started yowling. Caroline took out his carrier and set it down in the front yard, which was basically a patch of dirt. At least Crumbles could look around a bit from there.

Mia was right, the place was a wreck. It was a small stucco house, painted a rose color that was now faded and peeling. No one had lived there for at least twenty years, and before that first this relative then that relative had used it for a vacation or moved in for a few months before they got sick of the ten-mile drive for groceries, the hot wind, the huge humiliating sky, the coyotes yip-yipping with no consideration that a person had to get some sleep. A rusty porch swing sat out front, the squeaky kind with white aluminum poles and flowered cushions, now covered with several layers of dust and stained by generations of fruit punch and beer that never got properly cleaned up. That swing would have to go.

Someone had left several small pots of succulents, which seemed redundant in the desert, but they were thriving, so Caroline let them be, making a mental note to put them in some kind of arrangement later. A small wooden table stood next to a Weber grill, not the electric or propane kind. Caroline felt a little nervous to pick up the lid, so she just left it alone. Another mental note: Look under the lid when you're feeling stronger. She glanced at the garage, separate from the house and painted the same faded rose color, but decided to leave that for later too. She could only take on so much the first day.

Caroline stopped inside the door and looked around. The place didn't look half as bad as she thought it would. The walls could use a coat of paint. Luckily, she had kept paying the utility bill all these years, ever since Grandma Shipley died, so the lights worked. It was your basic 1920s bungalow with two bedrooms. In the front part of the house was a living room, with a kitchen stuck at one end. The kitchen had a sink and range—all dinged up and grimy-- and a four-seater table smack in the middle. The fridge stood by itself against the back wall, humming away, unconcerned by the absence of humans. In the living room, a plaid sofa with wooden arms sat opposite the windows that looked out on the desert. An old stuffed chair angled itself next to the sofa, with an end table and lamp in between. In the corner was a wooden case, about three feet high, with an antenna and several knobs. Must be an old radio. Cool. Caroline plugged it in and tried playing with the knobs. It seemed to be giving off a low hum, but she couldn't get any other sound to come out despite turning the knobs this way and that. Mental note: try again later, when you're more rested.

It looked like someone had squatted in the house for a while, but not too recently. Half a loaf of bread sat lumpy in the refrigerator, covered completely in green mold, along with a couple of cans of Coke. Caroline just closed the door. I'll deal with that later, she told herself. Aside from dust and spider webs everywhere, the house was pretty tidy, considering. Caroline picked up a sheet of faded yellow lined paper lying on the kitchen floor. It must have blown there from the table, either when somebody left or just now, when Caroline opened the front door. "Thank you," it said in scrawly handwriting. "I really enjoyed staying here but now I'm going." The ink looked fresh. There was no signature.

Caroline turned the sheet over. On the back was written, "For Dot, with love forever. Bert in sound thinks I'm going to marry him—haha." The faded ink was barely readable. Caroline squinted at it, pretty sure that was what it said. "Dot," Caroline said aloud. Grandma Shipley's first name was Dorothy, but no would dare to call her Dot. She put the note on the kitchen table for future thought.

When she turned on the kitchen faucet, it sputtered for a bit but then the water came blasting out. The water used to come from wells and her mother wouldn't let her drink it because of the arsenic. Luckily, now Victorville had grown enough that the house had squeaked its way inside the Water District boundary, so now treated water was pumped up from the aquifer and piped out by the city. Except for her mother, the grownups had seemed happy enough drinking the arsenic water.

"It explains a lot," her mother would say. What did it explain? Caroline wondered. Her mother never liked the desert and took a dim view of her mother-in-law, her friends and relatives.

Caroline fetched Crumbles from the front yard and plunked him down in the living room, still in his carrier. Then she walked down the hallway to check out the bedrooms. The walls were bare except for a photograph in a wooden frame. Caroline remembered it from when she was little. In the photo, Grandma Shipley, who looked to be in her thirties, stood in front of an art deco building, wearing a tweed skirt suit and a black tie. Her hair was pulled up into a tight bun, just as Caroline remembered it. Next to her stood a younger woman, maybe only slightly younger. She was dressed in a flowy dress belted at the waist. A jeweled barrette pinned one side of her hair back. Caroline squinted at some writing in the bottom right-hand corner. *With Buckie at MGM.* While Caroline had walked by this photo a hundred times as a child, she had never wondered who Buckie was. She wondered now. Mental note: Figure out what was going on with Grandma and Buckie.

The main bedroom was bare except for an iron-framed double bed and small wooden dresser, some beer bottles scattered about the floor, and a package of gum in the top dresser drawer. The gum looked surprisingly new, but Caroline chalked that up to good packaging. Whoever had squatted here preferred to drink in bed, apparently. The other bedroom was empty. The bathroom at the end of the hall was disgusting. Caroline decided to tackle that first, to get it out of the way.

She felt proud of herself that she had packed cleaning supplies last in the U Haul, anticipating that she'd have to clean before unloading anything. She was exhausted from the last leg of her drive and decided not to finish unloading until tomorrow, but she at least wanted to get the place cleaned up enough so that she could put sheets on the bed and fix herself some breakfast and coffee in the morning. So she filled the Crumbles' dish with cat food, put in her earbuds, cranked up Bowie's *Let's Dance*, and set to work.

The next morning, Caroline woke up early despite having stayed up until 2 a.m. or so cleaning the house and unpacking what started out as a couple boxes but turned into nine or ten. She never found her sheets and blankets so had laid a couple of tablecloths on top of the bed and slept fitfully on the scratchy fabric, turning this way and that under her jacket and a throw that appeared in box #5. Plus Crumbles kept jumping up and walking all over her and she was too tired to put him back in his carrier.

Leaving Crumbles inside the house, Caroline took her cup of coffee to the front patio and looked out across the desert to see what she could see. What she saw was mostly just scrub brush, with a few houses way off to the south, little blocks of grey and brown in the distance. She remembered passing a house when she drove in last night, so she stepped out a little further into her front yard and looked north to see if it was as close as she remembered. Sure enough, there was a rambling property about a quarter mile up the road. The house itself was a hard to see because it was surrounded by a high chain-link fence, the kind with green metal slats that kept you from seeing in. Just the roofs of the house and what looked like a couple of outbuildings poked up above the fence. Caroline thought it would be a good idea to take a nice walk down the road and introduce herself to her closest neighbor. You never know when you might need some help, though Caroline had no intention of asking for it unless it was an absolute emergency. *Just let them know you're here*, said Mia's voice in her head.

After she finished her coffee, she unloaded a few more boxes, then put on her jacket and started up the road. It was February and actually pretty chilly. It had gotten downright cold during the night, another reason Caroline didn't sleep too well, and she had been too exhausted and disoriented to get up and turn on the electric floor heaters. Who knew if they even worked? As she walked, she started to warm up. She felt the air dry out and heat up as the sun climbed higher above the horizon. While she hadn't felt much of anything on the drive down, she started now to feel content, satisfied with her move. She was happy, even excited, to meet her neighbors and get a better sense of this area she hadn't been in for decades but that held so many memories.

As she got closer to her neighbors' house, she could hear some kind of machine noise, as if someone was using a chain saw. No, it was harsher, more like metal against metal, or maybe metal against rock. She came up to the chain link fence but wasn't sure of how to get in. She didn't see a gate. She started to walk around the property, looking for a way in. Finally, well off the road by now, she found what looked like a gate with a high latch. She reached up to try to pull it open, but just at that moment, she was startled by a furious barking of what sounded like three or four dogs, at least, big dogs by the sound of it. She backed away from the gate. The barking kept up, but she stood still for a while and eventually the dogs quieted down a bit.

"Hello?" she shouted, hoping to get the attention of the dogs' owner and make it clear that she wasn't a burglar or some other suspicious character. With the sound of her voice, though, the barking started up again, more furious than ever, and one or two of the dogs started hurling themselves against the fence, which rattled and shook as if it might split apart. Caroline backed up further, not sure what to do. The metallic grinding sound kept going off somewhere within the enclosed area.

Well, maybe this wasn't the best time to meet the neighbors. She tried to peer between the slats in the fence but could only see vague shapes moving this way and that, probably the dogs. One of them kept throwing itself against the fence, over and over. Caroline thought she had better leave before it got hurt.

After she got back to the house, she spent the day finishing up the unpacking. As she was carrying a bedside table into the house, she noticed someone walking down the road from the grinding-metal house. She put the table down and waited.

The person turned out to be a teenaged boy, about thirteen or fourteen years old. As he got closer, Caroline could see that he had dark hair that was gathered in a braid down his back. He was about five foot two, slightly built, a strange mix of graceful and gangly in the way he walked. He got as far as the edge of her front yard, then stopped and looked at her. He had rather striking green eyes.

"My dad wanted me to ask if you need some help moving in."

Caroline wondered how his dad could possibly see what she was doing over that high fence. "Well, I'm almost done, but, sure, I'd be happy for the help. I can pay you."

The boy chewed on his lip as if he was mulling something over. "My dad says I shouldn't take money. I'll just help you."

"OK, I'll respect that. I appreciate it. What's your name?"

"Marcus. Marcus Greenwell."

"Pleased to meet you, Marcus. I'm Caroline." She didn't see the need to give him her last name. She wasn't in a neighborly frame of mind as she had been when she started down the road earlier.

With Marcus helping, she was able to unload quickly. During one trip from house to car, he crouched down and made cooing sounds at Crumbles, who had been imprisoned again in his carrier so he wouldn't run outside. Marcus didn't look very strong but he lugged the heavy boxes without complaint and ferried them at a clip into the house. At one point, Caroline saw him stop and look at the photo in the hallway of Grandma Shipley and Buckie. He reached up and ran his finger along the frame, which struck her as a little odd.

"That was my grandmother," Caroline said, coming up beside him. "The one with the bun. She used to live here and I would come visit her. Sometimes I stayed a long time. Until I was about your age."

"Hm," he said, and went back out for another load.

"She had parties," Caroline called after him, "with lots of people coming and going. Hollywood people!" He didn't say anything but it's possible he nodded.

After they were done unloading the car, Caroline made Marcus a thick sandwich of turkey, cheese, and tomatoes she had bought at a supermarket in Victorville. He dug into it happily. He didn't seem to want to talk, which was fine with Caroline.

As he was leaving she tried to hand him a ten-dollar bill, but he waved it away and sprinted off down the road towards his house.

That night, Caroline took one of the kitchen chairs outside, turned off all the lights in the house, and sat looking at the inky sky, the spattering of stars, the pale abyss below them that was the desert at night. Coyotes howled off in the distance, then closer by. Instinctively, Caroline turned around to make sure her door was closed, with Crumbles safe inside. The darkness emptied her out and filled her at the same time. She thought of Miles, his round, boyish face. She had so many questions about him and also questions for him that now he would never answer. Why did he let himself lose control? Why did he hit her? Why did he drink if he knew he would end up yelling mean things and slapping her around? Why did she think sometimes he was the ugliest person she had ever seen and then the next minute she adored him? Why didn't she leave him sooner? Why did she still think about him? Why did he die without telling her how terribly terribly sorry he was for everything he did? She felt like a ferret was inside her chest, writhing this way and that. It wouldn't settle down into one thing or the other, hate or love or longing or grief or forgiveness or an intense desire for revenge. The coyotes yowled. They were just hungry. You couldn't blame them for wanting to kill things.

She thought of her grandmother, went inside and took down the framed photograph and brought it back outside, scooting out quickly to make sure Crumbles didn't follow. She sat down and looked at it. It was barely visible in the light from the waning moon.

She remembered the smells when she would first arrive at the house as a child, bursting out of her father's car with Mia—leather boots by the door, wool blankets, roast chicken and potatoes, red wine. She remembered how strict her grandmother was, how serious, her mouth a thin, tight line. Grandma Shipley was always pouring herself a drink. The stiff lines of her body would start to sag. She lurched around, dropping things, while her eyes got far away, as if she were watching a movie in the air. People would drive up in cars, laughing, and Grandma would pour them tall drinks over ice or red wine in round glasses. The people tilted into one another, legs thrown over chair arms, or they rocked in the porch swing, looking at the stars and each other.

Caroline remembered her father picking at his guitar in the corner, her mother closed up in one of the bedrooms with the radio turned up loud, Hank Williams or Tammy Wynette. Sometimes her parents would leave, and then Caroline and Mia would lie in the big double bed watching the moon through the window, listening to the grown-up voices, the creak and bang of the screen door, the car engines, the coyotes yipping in the night.

Remembering all this, Caroline noticed something, in the picture. Her grandmother and Buckie were not touching, but they leaned, ever so slightly, towards one another. Who was this Buckie anyway? She would have to ask Mia.

The next day, Caroline returned the U Haul in Victorville then went to the Safeway while she was there to get more food. She called Mia from her car.

"You're right, the house is pretty bad. But not as bad as I thought it would be."

"Good! You can get it in shape to sell. As long as you're there."

"Mia, I live here now. You don't get it." She hung up. No point in asking her about Buckie.

When Caroline got back to the house, Marcus was sitting on the disgusting porch swing, rocking himself back and forth with a foot on the ground. His hair was still tied back in the braid, though

165

stray hairs had worked their way out all over his head. He wore a red flannel shirt that looked about three sizes too big.

Marcus stopped rocking as Caroline got out of her car with her bag of groceries. "Do you need help with anything?"

"Well, I might. But isn't it a school day?"

Marcus looked down and started making the swing move with his foot again. "I guess."

Caroline went inside and left the groceries on the kitchen counter, then came back out. "Does your dad know you're here?"

"My dad doesn't like me very much. He thinks I'm at school."

Caroline thought about that. She wasn't sure she wanted to get mixed up with this family that had a bunch of crazy dogs and a fence you couldn't see through. Not to mention that grinding noise. She wondered if there was a mother in the picture. "Why do you think he doesn't like you?"

"He yells at me. He hits me. I hate school and he doesn't care. He wants me to play football like my brother."

Caroline wanted to go unpack her groceries but she didn't want to leave Marcus just sitting there. He really should be in school. "I think it's normal to hate school at your age. I'm sure your dad loves you. Hey, that swing is pretty gross. Maybe you shouldn't sit there."

Marcus didn't move. "It's ok. All the stains are old and dried up. How would you know if my dad loves me? You don't know him."

"Good point. I need to get rid of that swing. I just haven't had time yet."

"No!" Marcus grabbed one of the aluminum poles. "You can't! It belongs here. I like it."

Marcus sounded like he owned the place. Caroline had a thought. "Did you used to come over here before I moved in?"

Marcus scrunched his mouth up. "Maybe once or twice."

"Did you go inside? You can tell me, I won't be mad."

"Maybe a couple times."

"Were those your beer bottles? And your gum?"

"Oh, sorry. I didn't have a chance to clean up. I would have, if I knew you were coming." He sounded a bit put out, as if she should have notified him.

Caroline thought she should remind him he was too young to drink but decided against it. As if he didn't know.

"How did you get in?"

"Back window. I barely got out before you came in." He perked up at that, clearly proud of himself.

"Did you leave that note? The thank you note?"

"Maybe." Marcus grinned a bit. Then he got serious again. "I am sorry I didn't clean up. I'm not like that. I just had a bad couple of days." He sounded like a forty-year-old for a minute.

Caroline picked up one of the potted succulents. "Are these yours?"

Marcus sat up. "Yeah! I dug them up from the desert. The pots were already here." He started swinging harder, producing a rhythmic squeak from the rusty poles.

"Could you slow down?" Caroline asked. "That sound."

"Sorry. Hey, do you have a gun. My dad thinks if you're a woman living alone you should have a gun."

"No, I don't have a gun and don't want one. How does your dad know I live alone anyway?"

"There's only like four houses out here. Everybody knows what's going on. What if a coyote gets your cat? Wouldn't you want to shoot it?"

"I don't let him out. Hey, do you want to clean out the garage? I'll give you ten dollars."

"Sure. It's pretty cleaned out already. Not much in there."

How did he know that? Caroline went in the house, put away the ice cream and frozen peas, then came back out with one of the kitchen chairs. She put it down kitty corner to the swing and sat down.

"How did you get in there, Marcus?"

"Oh, there was just a padlock. I sawed it off. I borrowed the metal saw from my dad's shop." He sounded very matter-of-fact. "Please don't say anything if you ever see my dad."

He sawed off the padlock? Caroline took a couple of deep breaths. "I won't. Your dad must have a lot of tools."

"Yeah. He works on cars. And he builds sculptures out of metal. He's always making something."

"What kind of sculptures."

Marcus shrugged. "People. Animals. Pipes that sing in the wind. Stuff like that."

Yeah, perfectly normal, thought Caroline. She stood up. "Well, if the garage is already cleaned out, I don't have much for you to do. You should probably go to school."

Marcus stood up. He started to say something, then stopped. Then he said, "I hate going to school. I usually hang out here."

"I thought you said you had only been here a couple of times."

Marcus scrunched up his mouth. "Ok, I came more than that. Like every day."

"You came every day?" Caroline suppressed the urge to yell at him, but she sure felt like it. "If you came every day, what's with the moldy bread?"

"An experiment. Just because I hate school doesn't mean I don't like to learn things." Caroline couldn't tell if he was messing with her. "It's pretty tidy in there considering," he went on. "Don't you think? Most kids would have made a huge mess."

"Marcus, I think you should go home now. No, I guess you can't go home. Well, you have to go somewhere. I need to be alone in my house for a while."

Marcus grabbed onto the swing pole with one hand. He started to put one foot up on the cushion but stopped. "Ok, I'll go. But can I show you something first?"

Caroline sighed. "Yes, but I don't have a lot of time so let's not drag it out."

Marcus motioned for her to follow him to the garage. Caroline noticed as they got closer that the padlock was open but fixed to look as if it were locked. Marcus took it off and opened the door. It was dark inside. Caroline hesitated at the door. She couldn't see in and for the first time started to feel nervous about Marcus.

"You don't have to come in," said Marcus. "You can stay right there. I'll get it."

What could he be up to? Caroline stayed by the door, waiting. She could hear Marcus walking around inside the garage. Pretty soon, he reappeared. In his hand was an old blunderbuss shotgun.

Caroline backed up immediately.

"See, you do have a gun!" said Marcus happily. Then he noticed the look on her face. "Oh don't worry. It's not loaded." He cocked it to show her. She peered at the chambers, but didn't really know what she was looking at. She looked at Marcus's face. He was clearly proud at what he could show her, and, strangely, she trusted him then.

"This is an antique!" he declared. "My dad would love it."

"Well, he can have it," Caroline said. "I don't want it."

"No, my dad doesn't deserve it. It looks like Dot wanted it, even if you don't!"

For a second, Caroline didn't know what he was talking about. Then, she remembered that Dot was the name on the back of the yellow note paper. Marcus apparently thought Dot was her grandmother. It did make sense, even if Caroline had never heard that name in her life.

"I'll put it back," said Marcus. "It lives here. And really it's nothing. It's nothing." He looked at the gun. Then he disappeared back into the garage. Soon he came out and started off down the road, but turned around and came back almost right away.

"Can I pet your cat before I go?"

Caroline was really so ready for Marcus to leave. "Ok," she said, "but don't dawdle. I mean it."

Marcus sprinted to the house. Caroline waited outside. She knew if she went in, pretty soon she'd be offering him something to eat.

Marcus reappeared and headed off down the road again. "I'll tell my dad I came home sick," he said as he passed her. "I'm pretty good at throwing up whenever I want."

Caroline bustled around until Marcus was far up the road, then sank down on the swing. She realized she was exhausted, from moving, from Miles being dead, from thinking about her grand-mother and her parents, and from dealing with Marcus. She remembered this swing then in a way she hadn't before. She moved the swing gently back and forth with her foot, the way Marcus had done, and looked out over the desert. She noticed for the first time that the desert wasn't just barren dirt with a few bushes. In the diffuse afternoon light, she could make out a few Joshua trees, holding their arms out like puppets. There were small yellow flowers on some of the bushes and some graceful swooping plants that reminded her of the aloe plants she had given to her neighbor when she left Portland. Maybe they were aloe plants. Aloes were succulents and this was where succulents came from after all.

She must have fallen asleep because she gradually realized that someone was shaking her arm. When she opened her eyes it was dark out, and her neck hurt when she tried to sit up.

"Are you ok?" It was Marcus.

Oh god, thought Caroline. Is he going to be one of those kids who just keeps coming over? She was going to have to come up with a way to set clear boundaries with him.

She sat up, fully awake now. "Yes, I'm fine. Why did you come back?"

Marcus sat down next to her on the swing. "I wanted to show you something. Can we turn on the lights?"

Caroline rolled her eyes, knowing Marcus couldn't see her, but she got up and went into the house. She flipped on the light in the living room so they could stay outside but still see. She went back out and sat down next to him again. He had an open beer in one hand and a photograph in the other.

"No drinking," said Caroline. She took the beer out of his hand and put it down on the ground as far away as she could without standing up again. Marcus didn't object. He showed her the photograph.

It was an old picture, slightly faded, of a young-ish woman sprawled on the porch swing, the same one they were sitting on. Caroline peered more closely at the picture. It was Buckie from the framed photo in the hallway. In this photo, she was wearing pants and boots and a cowboy hat, which was tilted to one side. She had on what looked like a man's denim shirt with the sleeves rolled up. She was looking straight into the camera with an expression that looked playful and vulnerable and slightly hurt, all at the same time.

"See," said Marcus. "It's Buckie."

"Yes, I can see that."

"Do you think they were lovers?" Marcus asked.

Caroline looked at him in surprise. Why would he even think that?

"Look," he said, pointing at the photo again. "She must be looking at Dot."

"It's hard to see. I'll look at it tomorrow. Where did you get this?"

"It was in the garage, on a shelf. Just sitting there."

"Why did you take it, Marcus?"

He shrugged. "I don't know. You can have it back. It's yours."

"Well, yeah." Caroline held onto it. "Hey, Marcus, I thought of something you can do for me, something I can pay you for. You know that ten dollars."

"Yeah?"

"The old radio in the house. I can't figure out how it works. Do you think you can get it to turn on? Are you handy that way?"

Marcus stood up. "Sure, but it's not a radio."

"It's not? It sure looks like one. What else could it be?"

"It was out in the garage. I brought it into the house. It's a theremin."

"A theremin? What's that? And how do you know what it is?"

"Reddit. I posted a photo. On my dad's computer. After he was asleep. Some Russian guy invented it. It makes these weird sounds. They used it in movies in the old days, movies with space ships and aliens."

Marcus opened the screen door. "Let's bring it outside. We can use an extension cord. I've done it a bunch of times."

Caroline followed Marcus into the house. He opened one of the bottom drawers in the kitchen, reached toward the back, and pulled out an extension cord. He draped it over his shoulder. "Let's carry it out together. It's hard to get it out the door."

He went into the living room and plugged in the extension cord, then connected it to the black cord running out of the theremin. Caroline stood, feeling a bit paralyzed, and watched what Marcus was doing. Marcus looked up and waved her over. "Come on."

"Wait," said Caroline. She pulled out a roll of packing twine she'd stuck in a kitchen drawer, cut off a long piece of it, then tied one end around Crumbles' collar. She tied the other end to a kitchen table leg. She really didn't want Crumbles running off into the desert.

The two of them hauled the theremin out the front door and onto the patio. Marcus dragged it further out, onto the dirt yard, taking it as far as the extension cord would allow. Crumbles came out with them, secure on his twine leash.

It was fully dark by now, with a cloudless sky. The waning moon hung high in the eastern sky, surrounded by a halo of light. Stars spread everywhere across sky, making it look busy and alive. Beneath this piercing but distant light, the cactus and creosote appeared to float in water, rising and falling as Caroline squinted into the darkness, trying to capture something solid.

Marcus stood behind the theremin and bent over it turning some knobs. The living room light made him look ghostly and alien. He raised his arms as if the desert were an orchestra and he was the conductor, holding audience and musicians in that stillness before the first note. What was he doing? Caroline almost yelled at him to tell her what was going on, but something stopped her. She was sick of this kid and sick of herself for letting him rummage around in her own house. But he looked vulnerable there, silhouetted against the emptiness. It was hard to imagine him at a school desk, or on a football field. How could anyone hit or rage at this slight and intensely curious child?

Marcus held one hand poised above the wooden box. The other began to move in a kind of dance, as if he were drawing figures in the air. At the same moment, a thin line of sound emanated from the box. Caroline flashed right away on old movies with jerky spaceships and paper mâché planets. But those images faded. Marcus moved his arm and hand. The sound rose and fell in an eerie music that traveled in waves out over the desert. The sky, with its imperfect moon and clustering, hushed stars seemed alert, listening. Marcus moved again and Caroline felt the sound move through her jaw, her eyes, her rib cage.

Marcus turned to her, smiling. "You try it!"

Caroline hesitated. "Is this what that message is about, on the back of the yellow note paper?" she asked. "The one you left on the table before you climbed out the window?"

"Yes, it must be!" Marcus laughed. "The paper was tucked inside, when I took it apart to try to get it to work."

Caroline took her place in front of the box as Marcus moved aside. Crumbles brushed against her leg, then plopped down in the dirt, as if waiting for something. Marcus showed Caroline how to hold one hand over the curved antenna while waving her other hand to alter the tone and length of each note. At first the sound seemed wild and uncontrolled, having nothing to do with her. But gradually she figured out how to control it, to create a melody that she felt inside her trying to come out, a melody that scared her at first as it had the audacity to pierce the desert silence, the pulsing sky. But slowly she began to relax. She could feel Marcus there beside her, quietly cheering her on as he rocked from one foot to the other. She sent the ghostly electric music out across the creosote and lupine, the aloes and tilted chollos, the burrows of the pocket mice and sidewinders, the dens of the coyotes. With one hand she held the world on a string, while with the other she talked to the stars in this new language, to the dipping bats and nighthawks. And then she talked to Miles, briefly, in staccato notes. With one long, rising tone, she explained to Mia about the vast desert sky. And in a rising, falling serenade without end or beginning, she spoke to her grandmother, and to Buckie, who gave to Dot and now to Caroline, by way of a sad and insistent boy, this magical machine with its wordless ways, its arrogance, its singing that you could hold in your hand and fling as far as the eye could see.

—Naomi Thiers—

SONG IN THE DARK

Will you take *all* my youth, yank out
every pearl, leaving me stunned, mouthing
a garbled message in the dark?

How many friends of my heart
are dead now, or their bold strokes dimmed
(by you) to faded things flailing in the dark?

How can my tired spirit find companions
like that again, bright sisters
to laugh me through this falling dark?

My tarnished body will never
gleam like the ingot it was, to lure someone.
No. So, am I shelved, a box in a dark

basement corner no one goes to?
No one sees two faint glows—eyes.
I'm still looking out, singing softly in the dark,

for I must make noise or be buried,
must daub on color or be taken for a dead tree.
If I walk lightly, you can't catch me, your dark

cold hand will close on nothing, stayed
one more day. I'm buttoning my striped sweater,
now, finding earrings. It's a cold evening, dark

by five, but I can walk to the park. I see
an acquaintance there sometimes. There's that busker
I like. I'll clap for his harp in the early dark.

Carla Sarett

THE HEADS OF THE KINGS OF JUDAH, 1793

All the priests were jailed or drowned.
Twisted ropes bound and lowered
the twenty-eight Kings of Judah
from Notre Dame's portals.
A giant blade. Bloodless. Clean.
Louder than human bone.
The limestone necks were cut.

Tubercular women screamed,
ecstatic, when head after head joined
the filth in the Square.
Starving children kicked
those chunks of Kings.
The crowd danced and sang
of Liberty and Reason.

It turned dark and wet, drunken
men fell on their knees
and begged for Napoleon.

Centuries later, those severed
heads emerge, interred
in a plaster wall. Faces scarred,
noses broken.
Eyes scooped out.

But the crowns remain,
mysteriously, intact.
We cherish fragments of kings.
Fragments of a fragment.
A jawbone. A finger.

Voltaire's ghost laughs.
These Kings made pyres
of their own children. Still,
we need their eyeless heads.
They remind us how far,
how fast, how stealthily
all of us can fall.

MEDITATIONS

———————————————Samodh Porawagamage———————————

excerpts from **ALL THE SALTY SAND IN OUR MOUTHS**

TO COUSIN G.

We've all grown up
and you are nowhere

close to schooling, so late
that, even I, the youngest

of the lot, know how babies
are born. I do have permission

to take you to the road, and help
you count the cars. Correct when

you get a color wrong. Yup, the sky
is blue, that lorry is also blue, your sand

castle beige or brown. More sand? No, I won't
take you to the beach for sand

until you can run!

A PRACTICAL LESSON ON ATTENTION

Hills loom larger when one nears them. Humans diminish in proximity.
                              --Sinhala proverb

As we looked on
the water trickled

far into the horizon,
the beach now an endless

black paddy prepared
for the ploughing.

So the fish bellydancing
for water glistened in the sun.

Villagers fought each other
to split the new land.

Tourists sipped on
the sight with their tea.

Let's go get our dads
I said to cousin's smirk,

he having helped thirty
fishies into puddles

versus my five. I shouted for help
from other kids chasing

the gulls away. Sapumal asked
for my water bottle

then spilled it. A wave
pounded on the horizon.

We shared one glance
and ran, zig

zagging over and above
the leaping fish.

THE WRISTWATCH

I think I'm fine, and now that the parents
have arrived, the hospital can't keep me
another night under observation.

My favorite nurse unstraps my hands.
Nobody asks why there were restraints
in the first place. She, then, whispering
something unhearable, shoves
a bag of my stuff into mum's hands.

We can't go home yet. Others, too,
need to be found. *I'm very brave
for waiting a day like I did.*

It seems only mum, dad, and Raja uncle
weren't caught in the *thing*. Now that

I'm found, six more are still missing—
seven with the baby Nisha aunty
is carrying, I correct mum.
They agree and praise me for
my sharp memory, which is
no big deal when I can't
remember enough of yesterday.

I ask for the bag of my things.
A silence the size
of ocean blows into the car.

So I ask again.

"It's dirty, son," dad says. "Let's wait
till we get to the hotel. Oh, it's a new
place we think you'd like to see."

Once at the hotel
dad leaves to join the search party.
But it's just him, Raja uncle, and a friend
of them living nearby. Mum busies
herself with a Southern province map.

I untie the blue polythene bag. The knot
beats my wits. So I tear it open
to the stench of stale vomit on what
used to be my favorite beach clothes.
Mum rushes to shield me from it all.

She can be fast, but not too fast.
My wristwatch falls out, too. As she

takes me back to bed, I cling on
to it for a clue, like it is the last
straw my past depends on.

You're safe, everything's fine!
I hide the watch under my pillow and wait.
Mum won't leave me this time.

So I pretend sleep for long, and more long.
Mum finally leaves to hide
the bag somewhere in the bathroom.
I take out the watch. It, too,
hasn't stopped breathing

like my morbid heart. Drops of water
have seethed inside, and a bubbly mist
blurs the hands and numbers.

But it's dry. It's so dry that when
I press the dial to my face
another sun begins to dawn.

CASKET SHOPPING

Nobody knows to put a finger on his height
and then Uncle Two has the genius idea

"How tall are you?": me, who made it, to serve
as the perfect model for his best friend's

coffin. My mother insists I shouldn't go
with them to the casket shop, but now
I fear no death. In the car I imagine living
in one for the rest of my life. People

bending over me in respect. *A fine young
Cricketer. Hasn't even matured*

into shaving his face. Then somebody ruthless
shuts down the lid. The imaginary darkness comes

alive, slithers into my guts. I tremble, and yank
numbed feet to bump against the front seat.

Uncle keeps patting my head. Just one glass
these days assures him that I am the son

he hasn't found for a month. I stroke the model
coffin outside the shop too much that my father

quietly growls a reminder. I follow them for a bit
and stop over a casket just enough to put me in

for display. Infinite curves like mouths of death
swallow my finger along the pillow box. My lowering

head snuggles against the soft silk. Everything
blackens and I freefall towards a vague

light in the tunnel. Somebody grabs me from the dark
in Uncle's form. "Not dead! Sapumal, my son!

He's alive. Look, here he is! Just like that!
No need for a coffin!" Then my father's voice

wafts above my ear "Just a power cut. Don't stare
into the torchlight." It's not real that I'm alive.

ON THE FIRST DAY OF SCHOOL – SEVENTH GRADE

after the wave, the national flag
forgot to staff in half.
The school flag, somehow,
drooped to the wind. The prefect
who climbed the pole to fix it
fell down and wrung his arm.
We watched in the silence
of a covered distance: the beach

almost next door, and we'd never
be very safe, so my ears
had twitched to every sound, ready
to flee. A mate asked how to do
this curious thing
with the ears and I scowled.
Already at eleven

I'd mastered the art
of running while shouting
for others to join. I found
no shame to it.
For PT on the Cricket pitch,
I'd be running
even before the bat

would touch the ball.
The umpire warned me
as if he'd ever faced a wave
running amok, so I kept
my cool and smiled.
During the interval,

loudspeakers announced
another string of speeches
for the rest of the day.
A few hired workers
moved the flags
inside the stadium.
The lion roared to the breeze
in hurt pride, holding high
its tail. I thought how lonely
it must have been to hang
erect on a pole
and blow with every wind.
An alumnus minister

came hours late to deliver a speech
on voting in tough times.
He never glanced at us.
The opposition leader, too,
said something on disaster
and I realized the heaviness
attached to the school's prestige
wasn't weight. At practice

after school, the Cricket coach
rebuked me for having lost

a kilo and I wondered how
it drowned. Later, I slapped
my captain who was glad
we got an extra
month of holidays and still
couldn't see in his eyes

wee bit of the terror I felt
when the wave lifted me
above the trees.

RITUAL

Too cooked to write more tsunami elegies,
I sleep for the ghosts to return with stories
I can't find in research. They stab me in tiny
ripples. I practice lying in sleep, and pretend
I'm dead, too. Then, memory reconstructs
the oblivion of the beaches and beyond. Buddhism says
sudden death leaves a trail of suffering to wake. The sun rises,

I'm about to go on living another
dead life – wrapping my head around
its last moment. The mind plays many tricks. The sunlight
makes it look real: death smells are gone, no whispers
in the ear. I have been working for five hours. My pen
slips from my hand and rolls
into the purgatory under my bed. This precision
scares me. Once, I recorded me sleep:
I didn't flinch at night, but my hair
moved out of my head, and returned at four

AN INTERVIEW WITH
JOHN ROLFE GARDINER

John Rolfe Gardiner spoke to *Potomac Review* from his home in rural Loudon County, Virginia, 50 miles northwest of Washington, DC, at the foot of the Blue Ridge Mountains. The handsome, white-haired writer tapped on the desk he built for his study, creating a staccato rhythm behind our conversation, edited here for clarity. In November, Gardiner celebrated his 87th birthday with the news that Bellevue Literary Press will be publishing his fourth short story collection, *North of Ordinary*, in which "Tree Men" appears.

PR Congratulations on your new collection. You say it feels like a rebirth.

JRG Well, the *New Yorker* was taking my stories, but they closed their doors to me some twenty years ago. I had a story collection at Atheneum, then two books at Knopf. When they didn't want the next book, I went to Counterpoint which published two, *Double Stitch,* a novel, and my favorite, *The Magellan House* collection. For some years I haven't had a publisher, and my agent can't be expected to mess with short stories because there's so little return. Whatever success I had with short stories I placed on my own. Then to have them discovered by this wonderful publisher of quality books is sort of like a rebirth and up from the ashes. It's very difficult for anybody to get published these days. There are thousands of people wanting to be writers or poets and success may depend on someone you know who will suggest you to an editor but in this case, it was a cold submission and the pleasure of un-expected discovery.

PR   You've published sixteen stories in *The New Yorker* and six novels and now another success. But you've spoken about feeling like an imposter.

JRG   I think I always wanted to be a writer but I certainly never supposed that I could. There's always the fear that you're going to be seen to be something of a fraud or that you are in fact a fraud. Each fiction begins as a mystery—where is it going, will anybody want to read it—and there's always an editor looking over your shoulder askance at the manuscript and smiling. I don't know any writers who call themselves "authors," that have the pretension to refer to themselves that way. They'd say "I'm a writer" or "I'm a wannabe writer" unless they are so fluent and so gifted—say, John Updike, who was able to talk about himself as an author in the third person. There are only a few of those in the world, I think. If you're me you look at yourself with the humility of a lost soul when you face the blank page.

PR   So what gives you the nerve to write?

JRG   Stubbornness. Admiration for good writing. I want to try it in spite of the penalties that may follow.

PR   The imposter is a character you return to in your stories. In "Tree Men" the nameless narrator doesn't really have the skills to be on the crew.

JRG   The idea came from my experience working for a swimming pool contractor in rural Virginia when I was in high school. I had family backing and the men I was working with had nothing but the health of their own bodies to fall back on so there could be a natural resentment to me as a student and as somebody who was more fortunate in resources. They had a certain way of welcoming me in their own lingo and they saw that I would work hard but they also knew that I was separate. I could leave at any time, and they depended on it all their lives so that was my perspective in looking at the tree men.

I was on my way to my local village one day and I saw a tree climber working up in a locust tree next to the highway. I stopped and got out of my car and incredibly he was making warbling noises like a bird, whistling beautifully in a way that I'd never heard before. At first, I thought it was a bird and then I realized that he was doing this and I could hear him when the chain saw was off. That became the Embry character. When I was thinking about the joy he found up in the air, the joyous sounds of whistling in contrast with the misfortunes of his life, it made me think of Thomas Hardy's "The Darkling Thrush" which ends with those beautiful lines, "So little cause for caroling, Of such ecstatic sound." That was the way the thing sort of came together.

PR Was the Hardy poem sitting in your memory or had you recently come across it?

JRG In the Army on the midnight shift I memorized some poetry, in particular Yeats. But the Hardy lines were a gift of a liberal arts education. In high school, we had to be able to identify quotes from dozens of poems. As an English student in college, poetry seemed the be-all and end-all of creative writing. In ninth grade our text defined poetry as "the best words in their best order" and prose as just words in their best order. Pretty silly. But there were some apt mots too. "What is an Epigram, a dwarfish whole, its body brevity and wit its soul." Things you memorize at that age stick with you.

PR You attended Sidwell Friends High School in Washington, DC, then earned a BA in English from Amherst. That's your formal education, but you say all writers depend on earlier writers to teach them.

JRG There's a lot about other writers and stuff you pick up along the way. Margot Livesey's *The Hidden Machinery* is full of wise advice. And she shares her early mistakes—how too much research and irrelevant detail got in her way.

Flannery O'Connor said don't go rummaging around too much in your characters' heads.

Fitzgerald said, start with an individual and maybe you'll create a type—start with a type and you've created nothing at all.

Grace Paley said she didn't like doorknob turners. Writers who can't get a character from one room to another without turning the doorknob. She was famous for being able to switch from one generation to another or one character to another without an apparent transition, you just pick it up from the context of what you're reading.

The wonderful story writer Berry Morgan said, "If there's a problem with a manuscript, write about it."

I'm sure all writers have a list of other writers who have taught them.

PR Why short stories?

JRG Well, they can have just as much impact as a novel. Deborah Eisenberg once made the comment that the novel and short story both share the same fixed costs—situation, plot, character, revelation. You need all the same elements, but you can't be as loose and chatty getting them on the page.

I don't know how to tell you what makes a good story. Nobody can even define a short story or a poem for that matter. I think Housman said I can no more define a poem than a terrier can define a rat, but I think we both recognize the object by the symptoms it provokes in us. With the short story, the best you can say is it's shorter than a novel. How much shorter? You decide.

If there's anything you learn as you go along it's that you want to make your characters seem organic—the things that are said organic to the situation. You can recognize stories in which the author's cleverness is placed in the character without much relevance, trying to be interesting but the reader sees that all these observations have nothing to do with the truth of the character they're talking about.

There aren't any final rules because every one of them has an exception. They always say show don't tell but there can be marvelous creative narrative that advances a plot and reveals character. You don't want to hear the machinery of the plot clanking along with the writer telling you what happens next and next with no character or dialogue in sight. Fitzgerald observed that action *is* character.

PR What kind of writing do you like?

JRG I want there to be rules about reality. I guess I'm not a fan of magical realism. I want there to be life as I understand it or experience it, not as something that could happen in a world that doesn't exist. Have you ever read the collected short stories of V.S. Pritchett? He's so great at knowing different voices, different argots, at understanding situation and writing organically within it. Try reading the *Complete Stories of V.S. Pritchett*. Read "Passing the Ball," read "The Diver," read "The Camberwell Beauty"—all of them. It's sort of my bible of short stories.

PR You also find inspiration from your home county in Northern Virginia, a setting you return to in many of your stories.

JRG Northern Virginia makes a generous backdrop to write against. It's where I grew up and returned to after college, the Army, and some years in New York writing for a trade journal and in D.C. working as an editor. I started writing stories about a rural village like the one I lived in with its nosiness around a corner store and the hypocrisies and delinquencies that give a place its peculiarity.

Anybody living here has seen the physical transformation of a county quadrupling in population. Then there's been another trans-formation, even more intrusive—the steam clouds rising over data centers, a reminder of the cyber cloud hanging over everyone and the lost privacy of surveillance capitalism.

PR You've written lyrics about that –

Turns out he's been part
Of a storm up on high,
Already been sold
To the cloud in the sky…

JRG Those were lyrics for Furnace Mountain, a roots music band based here in Loudon County.

PR Your lyrics from another song speak to the history of Northern Virginia, a history that seeps into your stories.

In the heart of the heart of Virginia,
Before blue and gray mingled blood,
On the ridge that leads down into Georgia
Above the Potomac in flood,
A story past knowing or telling
Is blazed in the bark of the pines,
Where speckled trout swim in the highlands,
Where redbud and dogwood make shrines.

In the heart of the heart of Virginia
By soldiers' bones tangled in vine
The fox and his vixen take refuge
In caves carved by water and lime.
Below on the Piedmont's rich farmland,
The corn tassels gold in the sun,
Two rivers run through Harper's Ferry,
Where federals shouldered their guns.

In the heart of the heart of Virginia
A healing still waits for its time,
Long mem'ry hangs over the red clay
Where creeper and green ivy climb.
By the Great Falls where white water tumbles
On down to the Chesapeake Bay,
The spirit of Jefferson walks with John Brown,
Still looking for something to say.

Your novels are grounded in American history, too. The slaving
industry in pre-Revolutionary War Rhode Island, labor disputes in
a Tennessee mining town in the 1890s, a World War I family drama
unfolding in letters between France and New York, a Philadelphia
orphanage after World War I, and Northern Virginia village life

after World War II. Someone could teach an American history course using your novels as touchstones. Preparing for the publication of your new story collection, are you still finding time to write stories?

JRG Yes, but it's easier to putter around in my wood shop. I've been working on some chairs after the style of Sam Maloof.

CAROL BERG's poems are forthcoming or in *Gyroscope*, *Crab Creek Review* (Poetry Finalist 2017), *DMQ Review*, *Hospital Drive* (Contest Runner-Up 2017), *Sou'wester*, *Spillway*, *Redactions*, *Radar Poetry*, and *Up the Staircase Quarterly*. Her chapbooks, *Her Vena Amoris* (Red Bird Chapbooks), and *"Self-Portraits" in Ides* (Silver Birch Press) are available. Her poems have been nominated for Pushcart Prizes and Best of the Net. She was the winner of a scholarship to Poets on the Coast and a recipient of a Finalist Grant from the Massachusetts Cultural Council.

DYLAN BOYER is a writer at work on a book, excerpts of which have been published online and in print by *Gigantic Sequins*, *Chaotic Merge Magazine*, and *Fast Flesh Literary Journal*. His work also appears in *Suicide: An Anthology* (House of Vlad, December 2023) as well as several online magazines. In 2020 he completed an MFA in Creative Writing. He lives somewhere on the U.S. East Coast.

MARY BUCHINGER is the author of seven collections of poetry; her most recent books are *Navigating the Reach* (Salmon Poetry, 2023) and *Virology* (Lily Poetry Review Books, 2022); *The Book of Shores* is forthcoming. Her work has appeared in *AGNI*, *Maine Review*, *Plume*, *Salamander*, *Salt Hill*, *Seneca Review*, and elsewhere. She teaches at the Massachusetts College of Pharmacy and Health Sciences and serves on the board of the New England Poetry Club. You may visit Mary's website at www.MaryBuchinger.com

MARK BURKE's work has appeared or is forthcoming in the *North American Review*, *Beloit Poetry Journal*, *Sugar House Review*, *Nimrod International Journal* and others. His work has recently been nominated for a Pushcart prize. You may visit Mark's website at: markanthonyburkesongsandpoems.com

ROCHELLE COHEN lives in Silver Spring, Maryland, and photographs the natural world of the Mid-Atlantic.

PAT DANEMAN's poetry is widely published, most recently in *Mid American Review, Naugatuck River Review* and *Poet's Touchstone*. Her full-length collection, *After All*, was first runner up for the 2019 Thorpe-Menn Award and a finalist for the Hefner Heitz Kansas Book Award. She is author of a chapbook, *Where the World Begins* and co-librettist of the oratorio, *We, the Unknown*, premiered by the Heartland Men's Chorus. She lives in Candia, NH. You may visit Pat's website at patdaneman.com

MAXX DEMPSEY lives and works in North Carolina. They are working on their first collection of poems.

MATTHEW JAMES FRIDAY is a British born writer and teacher. He has had many poems published in US and international journals. His first chapbook 'The Residents' is due to be published by Finishing Line Press in 2024. He has published numerous micro-chapbooks with the Origami Poems Project. Poems are forth-coming in *The Oregon English Journal, New Contrast* (South Africa) and *The Amsterdam Quarterly* (NL). Matthew is a Pushcart Prize nominated poet. Visit http://matthewfriday.weebly.com.

JOHN ROLFE GARDINER is the author of six novels and three story collections. A winner of a Lila Wallace-Reader's Digest Writer's Award, his stories have appeared in *The American Scholar, The New Yorker, The Ontario Review, American Short Fiction*, and many other magazines. His stories have been chosen for *Best American Short Stories, The O'Henry Awards*, and *Pushcart Prize* anthologies. "Their Grandfather's Clock" appeared in the Fall 2022 issue of *Potomac Review* and, along with "Tree Men," will appear in his new collection, *North of Ordinary*, to be published in 2024. He lives in Unison, Virginia with his wife, Joan.

JEFF HARDIN is the author of seven collections of poetry, most recently *Watermark*, *A Clearing Space in the Middle of Being*, and *No Other Kind of World*. His work has received the Nicholas Roerich Prize, the Donald Justice Poetry Prize, and the X. J. Kennedy Prize. Recent and forthcoming poems appear in *The Southern Review*, *Bennington Review*, *Image*, *Grist*, *The Laurel Review*, *The Louisville Review*, *Red Branch Review*, and others. He lives and teaches in TN.

DAYNA HODGE LYNCH Dayna Hodge Lynch is a poet from North Carolina. Dayna is a Black femme who writes to explore life. Dayna received their B.A. in English, a minor in African and African-American Studies at Loyola University of New Orleans, and their MFA from Queens University of Charlotte. Her work can be found in *Rattle* (2021 Finalist for the Rattle Poetry Prize), *Kissing Dynamite*, *Rappahannock Review*, and other upcoming publications. Visit Daynahodgelynch.com for more

PAUL JASKUNAS is the author of *The Atlas of Remedies* (Stillhouse Press), a novella, and of the novel *Hidden* (Free Press), which won the Friends of American Writers Award, and of two books forthcoming next year: *The Atlas of Remedies* (fiction, Stillhouse Press) and *Mother Ship* (poetry, Finishing Line Press). His writing has appeared in numerous publications, including *The New York Times*, *America*, *Tab*, the *Comstock Review*, and the *Cortland Review*. He is on the faculty at the Maryland Institute College of Art, where he edits *Full Bleed*, an annual journal of art and literature.

BRYANA JOY is a poet, illustrator, & independent arts educator who has lived in Türkiye, Texas, and England, and now resides in Eastern Pennsylvania. Her poetry has appeared in over 50 literary journals, and her book *Summer of the Oystercatchers* is forthcoming with Fernwood Press. Since 2021 she has been teaching regular online poetry workshops to foster meaningful arts community and support writers. Visit www.bryanajoy.com or on Instagram and Threads at @_bryana_joy.

PETER KESSLER lives in Philadelphia. His stories have been awarded a Pushcart Prize (2024) and an AWP Intro Award, and have previously appeared or are forthcoming in *Chicago Quarterly Review*, *Catamaran*, *Bellevue Literary Review*, *Gulf Coast* and *GSU Review*, among others.

GUNILLA THEANDER KESTER is an award-winning poet and the author of *If I Were More Like Myself* (The Writer's Den, 2015). Her two poetry chapbooks: *Mysteries I-XXIII* (2011) and *Time of Sand and Teeth* (2009) were published by Finishing Line Press. She was co-editor with Gary Earl Ross of *The Still Empty Chair: More Writings Inspired by Flight 3407* (2011) and *The Empty Chair: Love and Loss in the Wake of Flight 3407* (2010). Dr. Kester has published many poems in Swedish anthologies and magazines, including *Bonniers Litterära Magasin*. Her work has or will be published in *On the Seawall*, *Cider Press*, *The American Journal of Poetry*, *Pendemics*, and *Atlanta Review*. She lives near Buffalo, NY where she teaches classical guitar.

KENT KOSACK is a writer based in Pittsburgh. His work has been published in *Exacting Clam*, *Bruiser*, minor literature[s], *L'Esprit*, *3:AM Magazine*, and elsewhere. Visit www.kentkosack.com.

JOSH MAHLER lives and writes in Virginia. His poems have appeared in *Tar River Poetry*, *South Dakota Review*, *The Louisville Review*, *The Carolina Quarterly*, *Miracle Monocle*, *Puerto del Sol*, *The Southern Poetry Anthology*, from Texas Review Press, and elsewhere.

CULLEN MCMAHON graduated from Yale University and earned masters degrees at Brooklyn College and Middlebury Bread Loaf School of English. His fiction has been published in *The Columbia Journal*, *BigCityLit.*, and *J Journal*. He is currently represented by Kathryn Green Literary Agency for his novel, *To Aspen*. He lives in Utah and Connecticut.

JORY MICKELSON's first book, *Wilderness//Kingdom*, is the inaugural winner of the Evergreen Award Tour from Floating Bridge Press and winner of the 2020 High Plains Book Award in Poetry. Their second and third books *All This Divide* (Spuyten Duyvil Press) and *Picturing* (End of the Line Press) will be out in 2024. They live in northwest Washington with the moss and mud.

ILENE MILLMAN is a retired speech/language pathologist who worked with children who learn differently for more than 35 years. She published two language therapy games. Millman currently tutors adult literacy students through her local Literacy Volunteers organization and also assists for Rock Steady Boxing, an exercise program for people with Parkinson's Disease. Her poems have been included in anthologies and journals including *The Journal of NJ Poets*, *Nell*, *US 1 Worksheets*, *Passager*, *Healing Muse*, and *Connecticut River Review*. Her first poetry book, *Adjust Speed to Weather* was published in 2018; her second, *A Jar of Moths* is due out in February 2024. She was nominated for a Pushcart Prize in 2022.

FASASI ABDULROSHEED OLADIPUPO is a Nigerian poet and the author of a micro-chapbook: *Sidratul Muntaha* (Ghost City Press, 2022). His work has been published at *Oxford Review of Books*, *Scrawl Place*, *Short Vine Literary Journal*, *Rigorous*, *Olongo Africa*, *Roanoke Review*, *Watershed Review*, *Santa Ana River*, *The Citron Review*, *Stand Magazine*, *Louisiana Literature*, *Ambit Magazine* and elsewhere.

LINDA PARSONS is the poetry editor for Madville Publishing and the copy editor for *Chapter 16*, the literary website of *Humanities Tennessee*. She is published in such journals as *The Georgia Review*, *Iowa Review*, *Prairie Schooner*, *Southern Poetry Review*, *Terrain*, *The Chattahoochee Review*, *Baltimore Review*, *Shenandoah*, and *American Life in Poetry*. Her sixth collection, *Valediction*, contains poems and prose. Five of her plays have been produced by Flying Anvil Theatre in Knoxville, Tennessee.

SAMODH PORAWAGAMAGE is a Sri Lankan poet who writes about the 2004 tsunami, the Sri Lankan Civil War, poverty and underdevelopment, and colonial atrocities. His poems appear in *Out of Sri Lanka* poetry anthology by *Bloodaxe* and other journals. *Becoming Sam*, his debut collection of poetry, is forthcoming from Burnside Review Press in 2024.

BETH BROWN PRESTON is a poet and novelist with two collections of poetry from the Broadside Lotus Press and two chapbooks of poetry. She is a graduate of Bryn Mawr College and the MFA Writing Program at Goddard College. She has been a CBS Fellow in Writing at the University of Pennsylvania; and a Bread Loaf Scholar. Her work has appeared in the pages of *Adanna, African American Review, Callaloo, Evening Street Review, Paterson Literary Review, Pennsylvania Review*, and numerous other literary and scholarly journals. She is at work on two new poetry collections: *Oxygen I* and *Oxygen II*.

JILL SISSON QUINN is the author of two books, *Sign Here if You Exist* (Mad Creek Books, 2020) and *Deranged* (Apprentice House, 2010). She is the recipient of the Annie Dillard Award in Creative Nonfiction, a John Burrough's Nature Essay Award, and a Rona Jaffe Writers' Award. Her essays have appeared in *Orion, Natural History, Ecotone*, and elsewhere, and have been reprinted in

Best American Essays and *Best American Science and Nature Writing.* Her fiction has appeared in *Gigantic Sequins.* A Maryland native, she now lives in Wisconsin and teaches writing and literature at Mid-State Technical College.

CARLA SARETT is a poet and novelist based in San Francisco. She has been nominated for the Pushcart, Best of Net, and Best American Essays, and is shortlisted for the Charter Oak Historical Poem Contest. Her poetry books include *She Has Visions* (Main Street Rag, 2022) and two chapbooks in 2023: *Woman on the Run* (Alien Buddha) and *My Family Was Like a Russian Novel* (Plan B, shortlisted for the Poetry International Chapbook Contest.) Carla has a PhD from University of Pennsylvania.

HANNAH SMART is a fiction writer and literary/pop culture critic. Her work has been published in or is forthcoming in *West Branch, The Harvard Advocate, The Boston Globe, Puerto del Sol, The Rupture, SmokeLong Quarterly, Cleaver,* and *The Sunlight Press,* among others. She is the founder and editor-in-chief of experimental magazine *The Militant Grammarian,* holds an MFA from Emerson College, and is a Ph.D. fiction candidate and writing professor at the University of Southern Mississippi.

ANNABELLE SMITH is a student at Franklin and Marshall College. She has received national recognition for her work in flash fiction from Scholastic Art and Writing. More of her prose can be read on *Every Day Fiction,* the *Afterpast Review,* and other journals.

SARAH STARR MURPHY's writing has appeared or is forthcoming in *The Threepenny Review, Epiphany, Baltimore Review,* and elsewhere. She's managing editor for *The Forge Literary Magazine* and eternally at work on a novel. She's a runner with dogs, kids, and epilepsy.

RICHARD STIMAC has published a poetry book *Bricolage* (Spartan Press), over forty poems in *Michigan Quarterly Review*, *Faultline*, and *december*, and others, nearly two-dozen flash fiction in *Blue Mountain*, *Good Life*, *Typescript*, and several scripts. He is a poetry reader for Ariel Publishing and a fiction reader for *The Maine Review*.

NAOMI THIERS grew up in California and Pittsburgh, but her chosen home is Washington, DC/Northern Virginia. She is author of four poetry collections: *Only The Raw Hands Are Heaven* (WWPH), *In Yolo County*, *She Was a Cathedral* (Finishing Line Press), and *Made of Air* (Kelsay Books). Her poems, book reviews, and essays have been published in *Virginia Quarterly Review*, *Poet Lore*, *Colorado Review*, *Grist*, *Sojourners*, and many other magazines and anthologies. Former editor of *Phoebe*, she works as an editor and lives on the banks of Four Mile Run in Arlington, Virginia.

ASHLEY WAGNER is a poet from Baltimore. She is the poetry editor for *Ligeia Magazine*, and her debut chapbook is out now with Bottlecap Press. Visit ashleywagnerpoetry.com.

STEVE WING studied Creative Writing at the University of Montana with Richard Hugo, William Kittredge and Rick DeMarinis, and has published creative nonfiction and fiction in such outlets as *The Seattle Times*, *The Montana Standard*, *The Pacific Northwest Inlander*, *The Iowa Review*, *Under the Sun*, *Salon*, and Terrain.org. In 2022, he independently published a book-length memoir: *Secret Geographies: Growing Up and Out of Butte, Montana*. Standalone excerpts of the memoir were published in *The Concho River Review*, *North Dakota Quarterly*, and *Under the Gum Tree*. In March of 2023, by invitation, he read the *Under the Gum Tree* excerpt at an event at the Association of Writers and Writing Programs Conference in Seattle. His most recent prior publication was in *Catamaran* (Fall, '23). He retired from his environmental consulting job in 2017, and currently lives in Spokane, Washington.

MARY ELENE WOOD has published short fiction and memoir in *The Missouri Review, The Capra Review, Midway Journal,* and *Club Plum Journal.* She has also published personal essays in *British Journal of Medical Ethics* and as a chapter in her book *Life Writing and Schizophrenia: Encounters at the Edge of Meaning* (Brill, 2013). She is currently working on a novel while living in Oregon with her partner Grace and two orange and white cats.